THE INDIA I LOVE

Ruskin Bond has been writing for over sixty years, and now has over 120 titles in print—novels, collection of short stories, poetry, essays, anthologies and books for children. His first novel, *The Room on the Roof*, received the prestigious John Llewellyn Rhys Award in 1957. He has also received the Padma Shri (1999), the Padma Bhushan (2014) and two awards from Sahitya Akademi—one for his short stories and another for his writings for children. In 2012, the Delhi government gave him its Lifetime Achievement Award.

Born in 1934, Ruskin Bond grew up in Jamnagar, Shimla, New Delhi and Dehradun. Apart from three years in UK, he has spent all his life in India, and now lives in Mussoorie with his adopted family.

THE INDIA I LOVE

RUSKIN BOND

RUPA

Published by
Rupa Publications India Pvt. Ltd 2004
7/16, Ansari Road, Daryaganj
New Delhi 110002

Sales centres:
Allahabad Bengaluru Chennai
Hyderabad Jaipur Kathmandu
Kolkata Mumbai

Copyright © Ruskin Bond 2004
Illustrations Copyright © Sandeep Adhwaryu/PhotoInk 2004

ISBN: 978-81-291-4178-1

Twelfth impression 2018

15 14 13 12

The moral right of the author has been asserted.

Printed at Parksons Graphics Pvt. Ltd, Mumbai

In the spirit of goodwill, tolerance and ahimsa,
I dedicate this book
to all those who come knocking at my door
in the middle of my afternoon siesta.
May they too discover the benefits
and pleasures of a good afternoon's sleep.

Contents

Preface

The India that I love does not make the headlines. The India that I love comprises the goodwill and good humour of ordinary people; a tolerance for all customs; a non-interference in others' private lives; a friendly reciprocation at all times; a philosophical acceptance of hardships; love and affection, especially in children.

That is on the human side. And there's the land itself. Forest and plain, mountain and desert, river and sea, all mean different things to me. The sea brings memories of collecting seashells along palm-fringed beaches. The rivers—some of them described in these pages—represent the continuity, the timelessness of India. The grandeur of the mountains, the changing colours of the desert, the splendours of the forest, and the riches of the fertile plains; all these I have loved, and have attempted to celebrate over the years, in the way I know best, using the words I know best.

The essays and poems in this collection will tell the reader something of what I feel for people, places and things. Some of those feelings emanate from my childhood, some from the present.

Although I have occasionally had to cover old ground, the writing has been new, the approach still fresh and eager for love and understanding.

Of the ten essays in this collection, seven were written during the last two months. Three are taken from unpublished material in my journals.

Most of these essays are of a personal nature; not embarrassingly so, I hope. Young Kapish Mehra of Rupa Publications wanted me to write about the family who chose to adopt me (or was it the other way round), and some of the people and places that have been dear to me. I have enjoyed writing about them, and about some of the things that have happened to me on the way to becoming (and remaining) a writer.

I do think I hold a record of sorts for having had the largest number of publishers, at least for a writer in India. A number of the smaller ones have fallen by the wayside—still owing me royalties, of course! Others, like Rupa, have continued to grow and put up with me. The encouraging thing is that publishing in India has finally come of age. Even in this age of televised entertainment, people are picking up books perhaps due to the wide range that publishers offer. More and more writers are getting published, and some are even making money. No longer do I have to hawk my books and stories in other lands. My readership has always been here, and now I can write exclusively for the Indian reader, without having to make the compromises that are often necessary in order to get published in the UK or USA. So away with sensationalism, away with the exotic East, away with maharajas, beggars, spies and shikaris, away with romantic Englishwomen and their far pavilions. No longer do we have to write for the 'foreign reader'. I can write about the people living across the road, and behold, the people across the road are sometimes reading my books.

It also gives me a thrill when I find that something I have written turns up in a Hindi translation, or in Bengali or Marathi or Kannada or one of the many great languages with which this country is blessed. The potential for a writer is tremendous. Multilingual publishing is still in its infancy, but this creative energy has only to be harnessed and properly channelled, and a literary explosion is just around the corner.

In the West, the fate of a book is now in the hands of the agents, the publicity men, the prizewinning committees, the media—almost everyone but the reader!

I like to think that in India, a book can still make its way into the hearts and minds of readers without all the ballyhoo and beating of drums that goes with the release of the most mundane creations, especially those written by celebrities.

I like to think that there is still a certain mystery about the success of a book; that, like *Jane Eyre* or *Leaves of Grass*, it can be ignored by the critics and publicists, and still find a niche for itself, and that you can never be certain what may happen to your children. In other words, that the fate of a book is still on the knees of the Gods.

December 23, 2003

Ruskin Bond
Landour, Mussoorie

One

Come Roaming With Me

Out of the city and over the hill,
Into the spaces where time stands still,
Under the tall trees, touching old wood,
Taking the way where warriors once stood;
Crossing the little bridge, losing my way,
But finding a friendly place where I can stay.
Those were the days, friend, when we were strong
And strode down the road to an old marching song
When the dew on the grass was fresh every morn,
And we woke to the call of the ring-dove at dawn.
The years have gone by, and sometimes I falter,
But still I set out for a stroll or a saunter,
For the wind is as fresh as it was in my youth,
And the peach and the pear, still the sweetest of fruit,
So cast away care and come roaming with me,
Where the grass is still green and the air is still free.

Two

Children of India

THEY PASS ME EVERYDAY, ON THEIR WAY to school—boys and girls from the surrounding villages and the outskirts of the hill station. There are no school buses plying for these children: they walk.

For many of them, it's a very long walk to school.

Ranbir, who is ten, has to climb the mountain from his village, four miles distant and two thousand feet below the town level. He comes in all weathers, wearing the same pair of cheap shoes until they have almost fallen apart.

Ranbir is a cheerful soul. He waves to me whenever he sees me at my window. Sometimes he brings me cucumbers from his father's field. I pay him for the cucumbers; he uses the money for books or for small things needed at home.

Many of the children are like Ranbir—poor, but slightly better off than what their parents were at the same age. They cannot attend the expensive residential and private schools that abound here, but must go to the government-aided schools with only basic facilities. Not many of their parents managed to go to school. They spent their lives working in the fields or delivering milk in the hill station. The lucky ones got into the army. Perhaps Ranbir will do something different when he grows up.

He has yet to see a train but he sees planes flying over the mountains almost every day.

'How far can a plane go?' he asks.

'All over the world,' I tell him. 'Thousands of miles in a day. You can go almost anywhere.'

'I'll go round the world one day,' he vows. 'I'll buy a plane and go everywhere!'

And maybe he will. He has a determined chin and a defiant look in his eye.

The following lines in my journal were put down for my own inspiration or encouragement, but they will do for any determined young person:

We get out of life what we bring to it. There is not a dream which may not come true if we have the energy which determines our own fate. We can always get what we want if we will it intensely enough... So few people succeed greatly because so few people conceive a great end, working towards it without giving up. We all know that the man who works steadily for money gets rich; the man who works day and night for fame or power reaches his goal. And those who work for deeper, more spiritual achievements will find them too. It may come when we no longer have any use for it, but if we have been willing it long enough, it will come!

Up to a few years ago, very few girls in the hills or in the villages of India went to school. They helped in the home until they were old enough to be married, which wasn't very old. But there are now just as many girls as there are boys going to school.

Bindra is something of an extrovert—a confident fourteen-year-old who chatters away as she hurries down the road with her companions. Her father is a forest guard and knows me quite well: I meet him on my walks through the deodar woods behind Landour. And I had grown used to seeing Bindra almost every day. When she did not put in an appearance for a week, I asked her brother if anything was wrong.

'Oh, nothing,' he says, 'she is helping my mother cut grass. Soon the monsoon will end and the grass will dry up. So we cut it now and store it for the cows in winter.'

'And why aren't you cutting grass too?'

'Oh, I have a cricket match today,' he says, and hurries away to join his teammates. Unlike his sister, he puts pleasure before work!

Cricket, once the game of the elite, has become the game of the masses. On any holiday, in any part of this vast country, groups of boys can be seen making their way to the nearest field, or open patch of land, with bat, ball and any other cricketing gear that they can cobble together. Watching some of them play, I am amazed at the quality of talent, at the finesse with which they bat or bowl. Some of the local teams are as good, if not better, than any from the private schools, where there are better facilities. But the boys from these poor or lower middle-class families will never get the exposure that is necessary to bring them to the attention of those who select state or national teams. They will never get near enough to the men of influence and power. They must continue to play for the love of the game, or watch their more fortunate heroes' exploits on television.

As winter approaches and the days grow shorter, those children who live far away must quicken their pace in order to get home before dark. Ranbir and his friends find that darkness has fallen before they are halfway home.

"What is the time, Uncle?" he asks, as he trudges up the steep road past Ivy Cottage.

One gets used to being called 'Uncle' by almost every boy or girl one meets. I wonder how the custom began. Perhaps it has its origins in the folk tale about the tiger who refrained from pouncing on you if you called him 'uncle'. Tigers don't eat their relatives! Or do they? The ploy may not work if the tiger happens to be a tigress. Would you call her 'Aunty' as she (or your teacher!) descends on you?

It's dark at six and by then, Ranbir likes to be out of the deodar forest and on the open road to the village. The moon and the stars and the village lights are sufficient, but not in the forest, where it is dark even during the day. And the silent flitting of bats and flying foxes, and the eerie hoot of an owl, can be a little disconcerting for the hardiest of children. Once Ranbir and the other boys were chased by a bear.

When he told me about it, I said, 'Well, now we know you can run faster then a bear!'

'Yes, but you have to run downhill when chased by a bear.' He spoke as one having a long experience of escaping from bears. 'They run much faster uphill!'

'I'll remember that,' I said, 'thanks for the advice.' And I don't suppose calling a bear 'Uncle' would help.

Usually Ranbir has the company of other boys, and they sing most of the way, for loud singing by small boys will silence owls and frighten away the forest demons. One of them plays a flute, and flute music in the mountains is always enchanting.

✧

Not only in the hills, but all over India, children are constantly making their way to and from school, in conditions that range from dust storms in the Rajasthan desert to blizzards in Ladakh and Kashmir. In the larger towns and cities, there are school buses, but in remote rural areas, getting to school can pose a problem.

Most children are more than equal to any obstacles that may arise. Like those youngsters in the Ganjam district of Orissa. In the absence of a bridge, they swim or wade across the Dhanei river everyday in order to reach their school. I have a picture of them in my scrapbook. Holding books or satchels aloft in one hand, they do the breaststroke or dog paddle with the other; or form a chain and help each other across.

Wherever you go in India, you will find children helping out with the family's source of livelihood, whether it be drying fish on the Malabar Coast, or gathering saffron buds in Kashmir, or grazing camels or cattle in a village in Rajasthan or Gujarat.

Only the more fortunate can afford to send their children to English-medium private or 'public' schools, and those children really are fortunate, for some of these institutions are excellent schools, as good, and often better, than their counterparts in Britain or USA. Whether it's in Ajmer or Bangalore, New Delhi or Chandigarh, Kanpur or Kolkata, the best schools set very high standards. The growth of a prosperous middle-class has led to an ever-increasing demand for quality education. But as private schools proliferate, standards suffer too, and many parents must settle for the second-rate.

The great majority of our children still attend schools run by the state or municipality. These vary from the good to the bad to the ugly, depending on how they are run and where they are situated. A classroom without windows, or with a roof that lets in the monsoon rain, is not uncommon. Even so, children from different communities learn to live and grow together. Hardship makes brothers of us all.

The census tells us that two in every five of the population is in the age group of five to fifteen. Almost half our population is on the way to school!

And here I stand at my window, watching some of them pass by—boys and girls, big and small, some scruffy, some smart, some mischievous, some serious, but all going somewhere—hopefully towards a better future.

Three

Boy in a Blue Pullover

Boy in a faded blue pullover,
Poor boy, thin smiling boy,
Ran down the road shouting,
Singing, flinging his arms wide.
I stood in the way and stopped him.
'What's up?' I said. 'Why are you happy?'
He showed me the shining five rupee.
'I found it on the road,' he said.
And he held it to the light
That he might see it shining bright.

'And how will you spend it,
Small boy in a blue pullover?'

'I'll buy—I'll buy—
I'll buy a buckle for my belt,
Slim boy, smart boy,
Would buy a buckle for his belt...
Coin clutched in his hot hand,
He ran off laughing, bright.
The coin I'd lost an hour ago;
But better his that night.

Four

Our Local Team

Here comes our batting hero;
Salutes the crowd, takes guard;
And out for zero.
He's in again
To strike a ton;
A lovely shot—
Then out for one.
Our demon bowler
Runs in quick;
He's really fast
Though hit for six.
In came their slogger:
He swung his bat
And missed by inches;
Our wicketkeeper's getting stitches.
Where's our captain?
In the deep.
What's he doing?
Fast asleep.
Last man in:
He kicks a boundary with his pad.
L.B.W.! Not out?
The ump's his dad!

Five

And Now We Are Twelve

PEOPLE OFTEN ASK ME WHY I'VE CHOSEN to live in Mussoorie for so long—almost forty years without any significant breaks.

'I forgot to go away,' I tell them, but of course, that isn't the real reason.

The people here are friendly, but then people are friendly in a great many other places. The hills, the valleys are beautiful; but they are just as beautiful in Kulu or Kumaon.

'This is where the family has grown up and where we all live,' I say, and those who don't know me are puzzled because the general impression of the writer is of a reclusive old bachelor.

Unmarried I may be, but single I am not. Not since Prem came to live and work with me in 1970. A year later, he was married. Then his children came along and stole my heart; and when they grew up, their children came along and stole my wits. So now I'm an enchanted bachelor, head of a family of twelve. Sometimes I go out to bat, sometimes to bowl, but generally I prefer to be twelfth man, carrying out the drinks!

In the old days, when I was a solitary writer living on baked beans, the prospect of my suffering from obesity was very remote. Now there is a little more of author than there used to be, and the other day five-year-old Gautam patted me on my tummy (or balcony, as I prefer to call it) and remarked: 'Dada, you should join the WWF.'

'I'm already a member,' I said,' I joined the World Wildlife Fund years ago.'

'Not that,' he said. 'I mean the World Wrestling Federation.'

If I have a tummy today, it's thanks to Gautam's grandfather and now his mother who, over the years, have made sure that I am well-fed and well-proportioned.

Forty years ago, when I was a lean young man, people would look at me and say, 'Poor chap, he's definitely undernourished. What on earth made him take up writing as a profession?' Now they look at me and say, 'You wouldn't think he was a writer, would you? Too well nourished!'

✧

It was a cold, wet and windy March evening when Prem came back from the village with his wife and firstborn child, then just four months old. In those days, they had to walk to the house from the bus stand; it was a half-hour walk in the cold rain, and the baby was all wrapped up when they entered the front room. Finally, I got a glimpse of him, and he of me, and it was friendship at first sight. Little Rakesh (as he was to be called) grabbed me by the nose and held on. He did not have much of a nose to grab, but he had a dimpled chin and I played with it until he smiled.

The little chap spent a good deal of his time with me during those first two years of his in Maplewood—learning to crawl, to toddle, and then to walk unsteadily about the little sitting room. I would carry him into the garden, and later, up the steep gravel path to the main road. Rakesh enjoyed these little excursions, and so did I, because in pointing out trees, flowers, birds, butterflies, beeties, grasshoppers, et al, I was giving myself a chance to observe them better instead of just taking them for granted.

In particular, there was a pair of squirrels that lived in the big oak tree outside the cottage. Squirrels are rare in Mussoorie though common enough down in the valley. This couple must have come up for the summer. They became quite friendly, and although they never got around to taking food from our hands, they were soon entering the house quite freely. The sitting room window opened directly on to the oak tree whose various denizens—ranging from stag-beetles to small birds and even an acrobatic bat—took to darting in and out of the cottage at various times of the day or night.

Life at Maplewood was quite idyllic, and when Rakesh's baby brother, Suresh, came into the world, it seemed we were all set for a long period of domestic bliss; but at such times tragedy is often lurking just around the corner. Suresh was just over a year old when he contracted tetanus. Doctors and hospitals were of no avail. He suffered—as any child would from this terrible affliction—and left this world before he had a chance of getting to know it. His parents were broken-hearted. And I feared for Rakesh, for he wasn't a very healthy boy, and two of his cousins in the village had already succumbed to tuberculosis.

It was to be a difficult year for me. A criminal charge was brought against me for a slightly risque story I'd written for a Bombay magazine. I had to face trial in Bombay and this involved three journeys there over a period of a year and a half, before an irate but perceptive judge found the charges baseless and gave me an honourable acquittal.

It's the only time I've been involved with the law and I sincerely hope it is the last. Most cases drag on interminably, and the main beneficiaries are the lawyers. My trial would have been much longer had not the prosecutor died of a heart attack in the middle of the proceedings. His successor did not pursue it with the same vigour. His heart was not in it. The whole issue had started with a complaint by a local politician, and when he lost interest, so did the prosecution.

Nevertheless the trial, once begun, had to be seen through. The defence (organized by the concerned magazine) marshalled its witnesses (which included Nissim Ezekiel and the Marathi playwright Vijay Tendulkar). I made a short speech which couldn't have been very memorable as I have forgotten it! And everyone, including the judge, was bored with the whole business. After that, I steered clear of controversial publications. I have never set out to shock the world. Telling a meaningful story was all that really mattered. And that is still the case.

I was looking forward to continuing our idyllic existence in Maplewood, but it was not to be. The powers-that-be, in the shape of the Public Works Department (PWD), had decided to build a 'strategic' road just below the cottage and without any warning to us, all the trees in the vicinity were felled (including the friendly old oak) and the hillside was rocked by explosives and bludgeoned by bulldozers. I decided it was time to move. Prem and Chandra (Rakesh's mother) wanted to move too; not because of the road, but because they associated the house with the death of little Suresh, whose presence seemed to haunt every room, every corner of the cottage. His little cries of pain and suffering still echoed through the still hours of the night.

I rented rooms at the top of Landour, a good thousand feet higher up the mountain. Rakesh was now old enough to go to school, and every morning I would walk with him down to the little convent school near the clock tower. Prem would go to fetch him in the afternoon. The walk took us about half-an-hour, and on the way Rakesh would ask for a story and I would have to rack my brains in order to invent one. I am not the most inventive of writers, and fantastical plots are beyond me. My forte is observation, recollection, and reflection. Small boys prefer action. So I invented a leopard who suffered from acute indigestion because he'd eaten one human too many and a belt buckle was causing an obstruction.

This went down quite well until Rakesh asked me how the leopard got around the problem of the victim's clothes.

'The secret,' I said, 'is to pounce on them when their trousers are off!'

Not the stuff of which great picture books are made, but then, I've never attempted to write stories for beginners. Red Riding Hood's granny-eating wolf always scared me as a small boy, and yet parents have always found it acceptable for toddlers. Possibly they feel grannies are expendable.

Mukesh was born around this time and Savitri (Dolly) a couple of years later. When Dolly grew older, she was annoyed at having been named Savitri (my choice), which is now considered very old-fashioned; so we settled for Dolly. I can understand a child's dissatisfaction with given names.

My first name was Owen, which in Welsh means 'brave'. As I am not in the least brave, I have preferred not to use it. One given name and one surname should be enough.

When my granny said, 'But you should try to be brave,

otherwise how will you survive in this cruel world?' I replied: 'Don't worry, I can run very fast.'

Not that I've ever had to do much running, except when I was pursued by a lissom Australian lady who thought I'd make a good obedient husband. It wasn't so much the lady I was running from, but the prospect of spending the rest of my life in some remote cattle station in the Australian outback.

Anyone who has tried to drag me away from India has always met with stout resistance.

Up on the heights of Landour lived a motley crowd. My immediate neighbours included a Frenchwoman who played the sitar (very badly) all through the night; a Spanish lady with two husbands. One of whom practised acupuncture—rather ineffectively as far as he was concerned, for he seemed to be dying of some mysterious debilitating disease. The other came and went rather mysteriously, and finally ended up in Tihar Jail, having been apprehended at Delhi airport carrying a large amount of contraband hashish.

Apart from these and a few other colourful characters, the area was inhabited by some very respectable people, retired brigadiers, air marshals and rear admirals, almost all of whom were busy writing their memoirs. I had to read or listen to extracts from their literary efforts. This was slow torture. A few years before, I had done a stint of editing for a magazine called *Imprint*. It had involved going through hundreds of badly written manuscripts, and in some cases (friends of the owner!) rewriting some of them for publication. One of life's joys had been to throw up that particular job, and now here I was, besieged by all the top brass of the Army, Navy and Air Force, each one determined that I should read, inwardly digest, improve, and if possible find a publisher for their outpourings.

Thank goodness they were all retired. I could not be shot or court-martialled. But at least two of them set their wives upon me, and these intrepid ladies would turn up around noon with my 'homework'—typescripts to read and edit! There was no escape. My own writing was of no consequence to them. I told them that I was taking sitar lessons, but they disapproved, saying I was more suited to the tabla.

When Prem discovered a set of vacant rooms further down the Landour slope, close to school and bazaar, I rented them without hesitation. This was Ivy Cottage. Come up and see me sometimes, but leave your manuscripts behind.

When we came to Ivy Cottage in 1980, we were six, Dolly having just been born. Now, twenty-four years later, we are twelve. I think that's a reasonable expansion. The increase has been brought about by Rakesh's marriage twelve years ago, and Mukesh's marriage two years ago. Both precipitated themselves into marriage when they were barely twenty, and both were lucky. Beena and Binita, who happen to be real sisters, have brightened and enlivened our lives with their happy, positive natures and the wonderful children they have brought into the world. More about them later.

Ivy Cottage has, on the whole, been kind to us, and particularly kind to me. Some houses like their occupants, others don't. Maplewood, set in the shadow of the hill lacked a natural cheerfulness; there was a settled gloom about the place. The house at the top of Landour was too exposed to the elements to have any sort of character. The wind moaning in the deodars may have inspired the sitar player but it did nothing for my writing. I produced very little up there.

On the other hand, Ivy Cottage—especially my little room facing the sunrise—has been conducive to creative work. Novellas, poems, essays, children's stories, anthologies, have all come tumbling on to whatever sheets of paper happen to be nearest me. As I write by hand, I have only to grab for the nearest pad, loose sheet, page proof or envelope whenever the muse takes hold of me; which is surprisingly often.

I came here when I was nearing fifty. Now I'm seventy, and instead of drying up, as some writers do in their later years, I find myself writing with as much ease and assurance as when I was twenty. And I enjoy writing. It's not a burdensome task. I may not have anything of earth-shattering significance to convey to the world, but in conveying my sentiments to you, dear readers, and in telling you something about my relationship with people and the natural world, I hope to bring a little pleasure and sunshine into your life.

Life isn't a bed of roses, not for any of us, and I have never had the comforts or luxuries that wealth can provide. But here I am, doing my own thing, in my own time and my own way. What more can I ask of life? Give me a big cash prize and I'd still be here. I happen to like the view from my window. And I like to have Gautam coming up to me, patting me on the tummy, and telling me that I'll make a good goalkeeper one day.

It's a Sunday morning, as I come to the conclusion of this chapter. There's bedlam in the house. Siddharth's football keeps smashing against the front door. Shrishti is practising her dance routine in the back verandah. Gautam has cut his finger and is trying his best to bandage it with sellotape. He is, of course, the youngest of Rakesh's three musketeers, and probably the most independent-minded. Siddharth, now ten, is restless, never quite able to expend all his energy. 'Does not pay enough attention,' says his teacher. It must be hard for anyone to pay attention in a class of sixty! How does the poor teacher pay attention?

If you, dear reader, have any ambitions to be a writer, you must first rid yourself of any notion that perfect peace and quiet is the first requirement. There is no such thing as perfect peace and quiet except perhaps in a monastery or a cave in the mountains. And what would you write about, living in a cave? One should be able to write in a train, a bus, a bullock-cart, in good weather or bad, on a park bench or in the middle of a noisy classroom.

Of course, the best place is the sun-drenched desk right next to my bed. It isn't always sunny here, but on a good day like this, it's ideal. The children are getting ready for school, dogs are barking in the street, and down near the water tap there's an altercation between two women with empty buckets, the tap having dried up. But these are all background noises and will subside in due course. They are not directed at me.

Hello! Here's Atish, Mukesh's little ten-month-old infant, crawling over the rug, curious to know why I'm sitting on the edge of my bed scribbling away, when I should be playing with him. So I shall play with him for five minutes and then come back to this page. Giving him my time is important. After all, I won't be around when he grows up.

Half-an-hour later. Atish soon tired of playing with me, but meanwhile Gautam had absconded with my pen. When I asked him to return it, he asked, 'Why don't you get a computer? Then we can play games on it.'

'My pen is faster than any computer,' I tell him, 'I wrote three pages this morning without getting out of bed. And yesterday I wrote two pages sitting under Billoo's chestnut tree.'

'Until a chestnut fell on your head,' says Gautam, 'Did it hurt?'

'Only a little,' I said, putting on a brave front.

He had saved the chestnut and now he showed it to me.

The smooth brown horse-chestnut shone in the sunlight.

'Let's stick it in the ground,' I said. 'Then in the spring a chestnut tree will come up.'

So we went outside and planted the chestnut on a plot of wasteland. Hopefully a small tree will burst through the earth at about the time this little book is published.

Six

Spell Broken

We crouched before the singing fire
As the green wood writhed and bled
And the orange flames leapt higher
And your cheeks in the dark glowed red.
Alone in the forest, you and I; and then,
Came an old gypsy to warm his feet,
And shouting children, and two young men,
And pots and pans and a hunk of meat,
And a woman who shivered and sang to herself,
And a dog of enormous size!

You were laughing and singing an old love song,
Sweet as the whistling-thrush at dawn.
Swift as the running days of November,
Lost like a dream too brief to remember.

Seven

Simply Living

THESE THOUGHTS AND OBSERVATIONS were noted in my diaries through the 1980s, and may give readers some idea of the ups and downs, highs and lows, during a period when I was still trying to get established as an author.

March 1981

After a gap of twenty years, during which it was, to all practical purposes forgotten, *The Room on the Roof* (my first novel) gets reprinted in an edition for schools.

(This was significant, because it marked the beginning of my entry into the educational field. Gradually, over the years, more of my work became familiar to schoolchildren throughout the country.)

Stormy weather over Holi. Room flooded. Everyone taking turns with septic throats and fever. While in bed, read

Stendhal's *Scarlet and Black*. I seem to do my serious reading only when I'm sick.

Felt well enough to take a leisurely walk down the Tehri Road. Trees in new leaf. The fresh light green of the maples is very soothing.

I may not have contributed anything towards the progress of civilization, but neither have I robbed the world of anything. Not one tree or bush or bird. Even the spider on my wall is welcome to his (her) space. Provided he (she) stays on the wall and does not descend on my pillow.

April

Swifts are busy nesting in the roof and performing acrobatics outside my window. They do everything on the wing, it seems—including feeding and making love. Mating in midair must be quite a feat.

Someone complimented me because I was 'always smiling'. I thought better of him for the observation and invited him over. Flattery will get you anywhere!

(This is followed by a three-month gap in my diary, explained by my next entry.)

Shortage of cash. Muddle, muddle, toil and trouble. I don't see myself smiling.

Learn to zig-zag. Try something different.

August

Kept up an article a day for over a month. Grub Street again!
    DARE
    WILL
    KEEP SILENCE

These words helped Napoleon, but will they help me?

Try cursing!

I curse the block to money.

I curse the thing that takes all my effort away.

I curse all that would make me a slave.

I curse those who would harm my loved ones.

And now stop cursing and give thanks for all the good things you have enjoyed in life.

'We should not spoil what we have by desiring what we have not, but remember that what we have was the gift of fortune.' (Epicurus)

'We ought to have more sense, of course, than to try to touch a dream, or to reach that place which exists but in the glamour of a name.'   (H.M.Tomlinson, *Tide Marks*)

October

A good year for the cosmos flower. Banks of them everywhere. They like the day-long sun. Clean and fresh—my favourite flower en masse.

But by itself, the wild commelina, sky-blue against dark green, always catches at the heart.

A latent childhood remains tucked away in our subconscious. This I have tried to explore...

A—stretches out on the bench like a cat, and the setting sun is trapped in his eyes, golden brown, glowing like tiger's eyes.

(Oddly enough, this beautiful youth grew up to become a very sombre-looking padre.)

December

A kiss in the dark...warm and soft and all-encompassing...the moment stayed with me for a long time.

Wrote a poem, 'Who kissed me in the dark?' but it could not do justice to the kiss. Tore it up!

On the night of the 7th, light snowfall. The earliest that I can remember it snowing in Landour. Early morning, the hillside looked very pretty, with a light mantle of snow covering trees, rusty roofs, vehicles at the bus stop—and concealing our garbage dump for a couple of hours, until it melted.

January 1982

Three days of wind, rain, sleet and snow. Flooded out of my bedroom. We convert dining room into dormitory. Everything is bearable except the wind, which cuts through these old houses like a knife—under the roof, through flimsy verandah enclosures and ill-fitting windows, bringing the icy rain with it.

Fed up with being stuck indoors. Walked up to Lal Tibba, in flurries of snow. Came back and wrote the story *The Wind on Haunted Hill*.

I invoke Lakshmi, who shines like the full moon.
Her fame is all-pervading.
Her benevolent hands are like lotuses.
I take refuge in her lotus feet.
Let her destroy my poverty forever.
Goddess, I take shelter at your lotus feet.

February

My boyhood was difficult, but I had my dreams to sustain me. What does one dream about now?

But sometimes, when all else fails, a sense of humour comes to the rescue.

And the children (Raki, Muki, Dolly) bring me joy. All children do. Sometimes I think small children are the only sacred things left on this earth. Children and flowers.

Further blasts of wind and snow. In spite of the gloom, wrote a new essay.

March

Blizzard in the night. Over a foot of snow in the morning. And so it goes on...unprecedented for March. The Jupiter effect? At least the snow prevents the roof from blowing away, as it happened last year. Facing east (from where the wind blows) doesn't help. And it's such a rickety old house.

Mid-March and the first warm breath of approaching summer. Risk a haircut. Ramkumar does his best to make me look like a 1930s film star. I suppose I ought to try another barber, but he's too nice. 'I look rather strange,' I said afterwards. (Like Wallace Beery in Billy the Kid). 'Don't worry,' he said. 'You'll get used to it.' 'Why don't you give me an Amitabh Bachchan haircut?' 'You'll need more hair for that,' he says.

Bus goes down the khud, killing several passengers. Death moves about at random, without discriminating between the innocent and the evil, the poor and the rich. The only difference is that the poor usually handle it better.

Late March

The blackest cloud I've ever seen squatted over Mussoorie, and then it hailed marbles for half-an-hour. Nothing like a hailstorm to clear the sky. Even as I write, I see a rainbow forming.

And Goddess Lakshmi smiles on me. An unprecedented flow of cheques, mainly accrued royalties on *Angry River* and *The Blue Umbrella*. A welcome change from last year's shortages and difficulties.

Perfection

The smallest insect in the world is a sort of fairy fly and its body is only a fifth of a millimetre long. One can only just see it with the naked eye. Almost like a speck of dust, yet it has perfect little wings and little combs on its legs for preening itself.

Late April

Abominable cloud and chilly rain. But Usha brings bunches of wild roses and irises. And her own gentle smile.

Mid-May

Raki (after reading my biodata): 'Dada, you were born in 1934! And you are still here!' After a pause: 'You are very lucky.'

I guess I am, at that.

June

Did my sixth essay for *The Monitor* this year.

(Have written off and on, for *The Christian Science Monitor* of Boston from 1965 to 2002).

Wrote an article for a new magazine, *Keynote*, published in Bombay, and edited by Leela Naidu, Dom Moraes and David Davidar. It was to appear in the August issue. Now I'm told that the magazine has folded. (But David Davidar went on to bigger things with Penguin India!)

If at first you don't succeed, so much for skydiving.

July

Monsoon downpour. Bedroom wall crumbling. Landslide cuts off my walk down the Tehri road.

Usha: A complexion like apricot blossom seen through a mist.

September

Two dreams:

A constantly recurring dream or rather, nightmare—I am forced to stay longer than I had intended in a very expensive hotel and know that my funds are insufficient to meet the bill. Fortunately, I have always woken up before the bill is presented!

Possible interpretation: Fear of insecurity. My own variation of the dream, common to many, of falling from a height but waking up before hitting the ground.

Another occasional dream: Living in a house perched over a crumbling hillside. This one is not far removed from reality!

Glorious day. Walked up and around the hill, and got some of the cobwebs out of my head.

That man is strongest who stands alone!

Some epigrams (for future use).

A well-balanced person: Someone with a chip on both shoulders.

Experience: The knowledge that enables you to recognize a mistake when you make it the second time.

Sympathy: What one woman offers another in exchange for details.

Worry: The interest paid on trouble before it becomes due.

October

Some disappointment, as usual in connection with films (the screenplay I wrote for someone who wanted to remake *Kim*), but if I were to let disappointments get me down, I'd have given up writing twenty-five years ago.

A walk in the twilight. Soothing. Watched the winter-line from the top of the hill.

Raki first in school races.

Savitri (Dolly) completes two years. Bless her fat little toes. Advice to myself: Conserve energy. Talk less! 'Better to have people wondering why you don't speak than to have them wondering why you speak.' (Disraeli)

Wrote *The Funeral.* One of my better stories, and thus more difficult to place.

'If death was a thing that money could buy,

The rich they would live, and the poor they would die.'

In California, you can have your body frozen after death, in the hope that a hundred years from now some scientist will come along and bring you to life again. You pay in advance, of course.

December

I never have much luck with films or film-makers. Mr. K.S. Varma finally (after five years) completed his film of my story *The Last Tiger,* but could not find a distributor for it. I don't regret the small sum I received for the story. He ran out of money—and tigers!—and apparently went to heroic lengths to complete the film in the forests of Bihar and Orissa. He used a circus tiger for the more intimate scenes, but this tiger disappeared one day, along with one of the actors. Tom Alter played a shikari and went on to play other, equally hazardous roles: He's still around, the tiger having spared him, but the film was never seen (and hasn't been seen to this day.)

A last postcard from an old friend: 'Ruskin, dear friend— but you won't be, unless you keep your word about lunching with us on Xmas Day. PLEASE DO COME, both Kanshi and I need your presence. It will be a small party this time as most of our friends are either hors-de-combat or dead! Bring Rakesh and Mukesh. Please let me know. I have been in bed for two days with a chill. Please don't disappoint.

Love,
Winnie'

(We did go to the Christmas party, but sadly, the chill became pneumonia and there were no more parties with Winnie and Kanshi, who were such good company. I still miss them.)

January 1984

To Maniram's home near Lai Tibba. He was brought up by his grandmother—his mother died when he was one. Keeps two calves, two cows (one brindled), and a pup of indeterminate breed. Made me swallow a glass of milk. Haven't touched milk for years, can't stand the stuff, but drank it so as not to hurt his feelings. (Mani and his Granny turned up in my children's story *Getting Granny's Glasses.)*

On the 6th it was bitterly cold, and the snow came in through my bedroom roof. Not enough money to go away, but at least there's enough for wood and coal. I hate the cold—but the children seems to enjoy it. Raki, Muki and Dolly in constant high spirits.

February

Two days and nights of blizzard—howling winds, hail, sleet, snow. Prem bravely goes out for coal and kerosene oil. Worst weather we've ever had up here. Sick of it.

March

Peach, plum and apricot trees in blossom. Gentle weather at last. Schools reopen.

Sold German and Dutch translation rights in a couple of my children's books. I wish I could write something of lasting worth. I've done a few good stories but they are so easily lost in the mass of wordage that pours forth from the world's presses.

Here are some statistics which I got from the U.K. a couple of years ago:

There are over nine million books in the British Museum and they fill 86 miles of shelving.

There are over 50,000 living British authors. They don't get rich. The latest Society of Authors survey shows that only 55 per cent of those whose main occupation is writing earn over £700 a year.

Britan has 8,500 booksellers, as well as many other shops where books are sold.

The first book to be printed in Britain was *The Dictes and Sayings of the Philosophers*, which was translated and printed by William Caxton in 1477.

As many books were published in Britain between 1940 and 1980 as in the five centuries from Caxton's first book.

Who says the reading habit is dying?

April

The 'adventure wind' of my boyhood—I felt it again today. Walked five miles to Suakholi, to look at an infinity of mountains.

The feeling of space—limitless space—can only be experienced by living in the mountains.

It is the emotional, the spiritual surge, that draws us back to the mountains again and again. It was not altogether a matter of mysticism or religion that prompted the ancients to believe that their gods dwelt in the high places of this earth. Those gods, by whatever name we know them, still dwell there. From time to time we would like to be near them, that we may know them and ourselves more intimately.

May

Completed my half-century and launched into my 51st year.

Fifty is a dangerous age for most men. Last year there was nothing to celebrate, and at the end of it, my diary went into the dustbin. There was an abortive and unhappy love affair (dear reader, don't fall in love at fifty!), a crisis in the home (with Prem missing for weeks), conflicts with publishers, friends, myself. So skip being fifty. Become fifty-one as soon as possible; you will find yourself in calmer waters. If you fall in love at the age of fifty, inner turmoil and disappointment is almost guaranteed. Don't listen to what the wise men say about love. P.G. Wodehouse said the whole thing more succinctly: 'You know, the way love can change a fellow is really frightful to contemplate.' Especially when a fifty-year -old starts behaving like a sixteen-year-old!

Most of my month's earnings went to the dentist. And I notice he's wearing a new suit.

June

A name—a lovely face—turn back the years: 45 years to be exact, when I was a small boy in Jamnagar, where my father taught English to some of the younger princes and princesses—among them M—, whose picture I still have in my album (taken by my father). She wrote to me after reading something I'd written, wanting to know if I was the same little boy, i.e., Mr. Bond's mischievous son. I responded, of course. A link with my father is so rare; and besides, I had a crush on her. My first love! So long ago—but it seems like yesterday...

Monsoon breaks.

Money-drought breaks.

And if there's a connection, may the rain gods be generous this year.

(The rest of the year's entries were fairly mundane, implying that life at Ivy Cottage, Landour, went on pretty smoothly. But the rain gods played a trick or two. Although they were fairly generous to begin with, the year ended with a drought, as my mid-December entry indicates: 'Dust covers everything, after nearly two and half months of dry weather. Clouds build up, but disperse.' Always receptive to Nature's unpredictability, I wrote my story *'Dust on the Mountain'*.)

1985

On the flyleaf of this year's diary are written two maxims: 'Pull your own strings' and 'Act impeccably'. I'm not sure that I did either with much success, but I did at least try. And trying is what it's all about...

January

My book of poems and prayers finally published by Thomson Press, seven years after acceptance. Received a copy. Hope it won't be the only one. Splendid illustrations by Suddha. (Shortly afterwards, Thomson Press closed down their children's book division and my book vanished too!)

Can thought (consciousness) exist outside the body? Can it be trained to do so? Can its existence continue after the body has gone? Does it need a body? (but without a body it would have nothing to do.)

Of course thoughts can travel. But do they travel of their own volition, or because of the bodily energy that sustains them?

We have the wonders of clairvoyance, of presentiments, and premonitions in dreams. How to account for these?

Our thinking is conditioned by past experience (including the past experience of the human race), and so, as Bergson said: 'We think with only a small part of the past, but it is with our entire past, including the original bent of the soul, that we desire, will, and act.'

'The original bent of the soul...' I accept that man has a soul, or he would be incapable of compassion.

February

We move from mind to matter:

Tried a pizza—seemed to take an hour to travel down my gullet.

Two days later: Swiss cheese pie with Mrs Goel who's Swiss—and more adventures of the digestive tract.

Next day: Supper with the Deutschmanns from Australia. Australian pie.

Following day: Rest and recovery. Then reverted to good old dal-*bhaat*.

Accompanied N— to Dehradun and ended up paying for our lunch. The trouble with rich people is that they never seem to have any money on them. That's how they stay rich, I suppose.

March

Sold *A Crow for All Seasons* to the Children's Film Society for a small sum. They think it will make a good animated film. And so it will. But I'm pretty sure they won't make it. They have forgotten about the story they bought from me five years ago! (Neither film was ever made.)

April

The wind in the pines and deodars hums and moans, but in the chestnut it rustles and chatters and makes cheerful conversation. The horse-chestnut in full leaf is a magnificent sight.

Children down with mumps. I go down with a viral fever for two days. Recover and write three articles. Hope for the best. It is not in mortals to command success.

✧

Men get their sensual natures from their mothers, their intellectual make-up from their fathers; women, the other way round, (or so I'm told!)

June

Not many years ago you had to walk for weeks to reach the pilgrim destinations—Badrinath, Gangotri, Kedarnath, Tungnath... Last week, within a few days, I covered them all, as most of them are now accessible by motorable road. I liked some of the smaller places, such as Nandprayag, which are still unspoilt. Otherwise, I'm afraid the dhaba-culture of urban India has followed the cars and buses into the mountains and up to the shrines.

July

The deodar (unlike the pine) is a hospitable tree. It allows other things to grow beneath it, and it tolerates growth upon its trunk and branches—moss, ferns, small plants. The tiny young cones are like blossoms on the dark green foliage at this time of the year.

Slipped and cracked my head against the grid of a truck. Blood gushed forth, so I dashed across to Dr. Joshi's little clinic and had three stitches and an anti-tetanus shot. Now you know why I don't travel well.

M.C. Beautiful, seductive. 'She walks in beauty like the night...'

August

Endless rain. No sun for a week. But M.C. playful, loving. In good spirits, I wrote a funny story about cricket. I'd find it hard to write a serious story about cricket. The farcical element appeals to me more then the 'nobler' aspects of the game. Uncle Ken made more runs with his pads than with his bat. And out of every ten catches that came his way, he took one!

October

Paid rent in advance for next year; paid school fees to end of this year. Broke, but don't owe a paisa to a soul. Ice cream in town with Raki. Came home to find a couple of cheques waiting for me!

M. C. is quick as a vixen, but makes the chase worthwhile. We walk in the wind and the rain. Exhilarating.

Frantic kisses.
Time to say goodbye!
When love is swiftly stolen,
It hasn't time to die.

When in love, I'm inspired to write bad verse.

Teilhard de Chardin said it better:

'Some day, after we have mastered the winds, the Waves, the tides and gravity, we shall harness for God the energies of love. Then for the second time in the history of the world, man will have discovered fire.'

February 1986

Destiny is really the strength of our desires.

Raki back from the village. I'm happy he has made himself popular there, adapted to both worlds, the comparative sophistication of Mussoorie and the simple earthiness of village Bachhanshu in the remoteness of Garhwal. Being able to get on with everyone, rich or poor, old or young, makes life so much easier. Or so I've found! My parents' broken marriage, father's early death, and the difficulties of adapting to my stepfather's home, resulted in my being something of a loner until I was thirty. Now I've become a family person without marrying. Selfish?

Returned to two great comic novels—H. G. Wells's *History of Mr. Polly* and George and Weedon Grossmith's *Diary of a Nobody. Polly* has some marvellous set pieces, while *Nobody* never fails to make me laugh.

M. C. returns with a spring in the springtime. The same good nature and sense of humour.

> 'Three things in love the foolish will desire:
> Faith, constancy, and passion; but the wise

Only an hour's happiness require
And not to look into uncaring eyes.'
(Kenneth Hopkins)

March

Getting Granny's Glasses received a nomination for the Carnegie Medal. *Cricket for the Crocodile* makes friends.

After a cold wet spell, Holi brings warmer days, ladybirds, new friends.

May

So now I'm 52. Time to pare life down to the basics of doing.

a) what I have to do

b) what I want to do

Much prefer the latter.

June

Blood pressure up and down.

Writing for a living:

It's a battlefield!

People do ask funny questions. Accosted on the road by a stranger, who proceeds to cross-examine me, starting with: 'Excuse me, are you a good writer?' For once, I'm stumped for an answer.

Muki no better. Bangs my study door, sees me give a start, and says: 'This door makes a lot of noise, doesn't it?'

August

Thousands converge on the town from outlying villages, for local festival. By late evening, scores of drunks staggering about on the road. A few fights, but largely good-natured.

The women dress very attractively and colourfully. But for most of the menfolk, the height of fashion appears to be a new pyjama-suit. But I'm a pyjama person myself. Pyjamas are comfortable, I write better wearing pyjamas!

September

Month began with a cheque that bounced. Refrained from checking my blood pressure.

Monsoon growth at its peak. The ladies' slipper orchids are tailing off, but I noticed all the following wild flowers: Balsam (two kinds), commelina, agrimony, wild geranium (very pretty), sprays of white flowers emanating from the wild ginger, the scarlet fruit of the cobra lily just forming tiny mushrooms set like pearls in a retaining wall; ferns still green, which means more rain to come; escaped dahlias everywhere; wild begonias and much else. The best time of year for wild flowers.

February 1987

Home again, after five days in hospital with bleeding ulcers. Loving care from Prem. Support from Ganesh and others. Nurse Nirmala very caring. I prefer nurses to doctors. Milk, hateful milk!

After a week, back in hospital. Must have been all that milk. Or maybe Nurse Nirmala!

March

To Delhi for a check-up. Public gardens ablaze with flowers. Felt much better.

'A merry heart does good like a medicine, but a broken spirit dries the bones.'

'He who tenderly brings up his servant from a child, shall have him become his son at the end.'

(Book of Proverbs)

May

Lines for future use:

Lunch (at my convent school) was boiled mutton and overcooked pumpkin, which made death lose some of its sting.

Pictures on the wall are not just something to look at. After a time, they become company.

Another bus accident, and a curious crowd gathered with disaster-inspired speed.

He (Upendra) has a bonfire of a laugh.

(Forgot to use these lines, so here they are!)

May

Ordered a birthday cake, but it failed to arrive. Sometimes I think inertia is the greatest force in the world.

Wrote a ghost story, something I enjoy doing from time to time, although I must admit that, try as I might, I have yet to encounter a supernatural being. Unless you can count dreams as being supernatural experiences.

August

After the drought, the deluge.

Landslide near the house. It rumbled away all night and I kept getting up to see how close it was getting to us. About twenty feet away. The house is none too stable, badly in need of repairs. In fact, it looks a bit like the Lucknow Residency after the rebels had finished shelling it.

(It did, however, survive the landslide, although the retaining wall above our flat collapsed, filling the sitting room with rubble.)

November

To Delhi, to receive a generous award from Indian Council for Child Education. Presented to me by the Vice-President of India. Got back to my host's home to discover that the envelope contained another awardee's cheque. He was due to leave for Ahmedabad by train. Rushed to railway station, to find him on the platform studying my cheque which he had just discovered in his pocket. Exchanged cheques. All's well that ends well.

A Delhi Visit

A long day's taxi journey to Delhi. It gets tiring towards the end, but I have always found the road journey interesting and at times quite enchanting—especially the rural scene from outside Dehradun, through Roorkee and various small wayside towns, up to Muzzafarnagar and the outskirts of Meerut: the sugar cane being harvested and taken to the sugar factories (by cart or truck); the fruit on sale everywhere (right now, its the season for bananas and 'chakotra' lemons); children bathing in small canals; the serenity of mango groves...

Of course there's the other side to all this—the litter that accumulates wherever there are large centres of population; the blaring of horns; loudspeakers here and there. It's all part of the picture. But the picture as a whole is a fascinating one, and the colours can't be matched anywhere else.

Marigolds blaze in the sun. Yes, whole fields of them, for they are much in demand on all sorts of ceremonial occasions: Marriages, temple pujas, and garlands for dignitaries—making the humble marigold a good cash crop.

And not so humble after all. For although the rose may still be the queen of flowers, and the jasmine the princess of fragrance, the marigold holds its own through sheer sturdiness, colour and cheerfulness. It is a cheerful flower, no doubt about that—brightening up winter days, often when there is little else in bloom. It doesn't really have a fragrance—simply an acid odour, not to everyone's liking—but it has a wonderful range of colour, from lower yellow to deep orange to golden bronze, especially among the giant varieties in the hills.

Otherwise this is not a great month for flowers, although at the India International Centre (IIC) in Delhi, where I am staying, there is a pretty tree with fragile pink flowers—the Chorisnia speciosa, each bloom having five large pink petals, with long pistula.

Eight

Garhwal Himalaya

Deep in the crouching mist lie the mountains.
Climbing the mountains are forests
Of rhododendron, spruce and deodar—
Trees of God, we call them—sighing
In the wind from the passes of Garhwal;
And the snow leopard moans softly
Where the herdsmen pass, their lean sheep cropping
Short winter grass.

And clinging to the sides of the mountains,
The small stone houses of Garhwal;
Then thin fields of calcinated soil torn
From the old spirit-haunted rocks;
Pale women plough, they laugh at the thunder,
And their men go down to the plains:
Little grows on the beautiful mountains
In the north wind.

There is hunger of children at noon; yet
There are those who sing of sunsets
And the gods and glories of Himachal,
Forgetting no one eats sunsets.
Wonder, then, at the absence of old men;
For some grow old at their mother's breasts,
In cold Garhwal.

Nine

The India I Carried with Me

I AM NOW GOING BACK IN TIME, TO A PERIOD
when I was caught between East and West, and had to make
up my mind just where I belonged. I had been away from
India for barely a month before I was longing to return.
The insularity of the place where I found myself (Jersey,
in the Channel Islands) had something to do with it, I
suppose. There was little there to remind me of India or the
East, not one brown face to be seen in the streets or on the
beaches. I'm sure it's a different sort of place now; but fifty
years ago it had nothing to offer by way of companionship or
good cheer to a lonely, sensitive boy who had left home and
friends in search of a 'better future'.

I had come to England with a dream of sorts, and I was to
return to India with another kind of dream; but in between
there were to be four years of dreary office work, lonely

bed-sitting rooms, shabby lodging houses, cheap snack bars, hospital wards, and the struggle to write my first book and find a publisher for it.

I started work in a large departmental store called LeRiche. At eight in the morning, when I walked to the store, it was dark. At six in the evening, when I walked home, it was dark again. Where were all those sunny beaches Jersey was famous for? I would have to wait for summer to see them, and a Saturday afternoon to take a dip in the sea.

Occasionally, after an early supper, I would walk along the deserted seafront. If the tide was in and the wind approaching gale-force, the waves would climb the sea wall and drench me with their cold salt spray. My aunt, with whom I was staying, thought I was quite mad to take this solitary walk; but I have always been at one with nature, even in its wilder moments, and the wind and the crashing waves gave me a sense of freedom, strengthened my determination to escape from the island and go my own way.

When I wasn't walking along the seafront, I would sit at the portable typewriter in my small attic room, and hammer out the rough chapters of the book that was to become my first novel. These were characters and incidents based on the journal I had kept during my last year in India. It was 1951, recalled in late 1952. An eighteen-year-old looking back on incidents in the life of a seventeen-year-old! Nostalgia and longing suffused those pages. How I longed to be back with my friends in the small town of Dehradun—a leafy place, sunny, fruit-laden, easy-going; every familiar corner etched clearly in my memory. Somehow, it had been that last year in Dehra that had brought me closer to the India that I had so far only taken for granted.

An India of close and sometimes sentimental friendships. Of striking contrasts: A small cinema showing English pictures (a George Formby comedy or an American musical) and only a couple of hours away thousands taking a dip in the sacred water of the Ganga. Or outside the station, hundreds of pony-drawn tongas waiting to pick up passengers, while the more affluent climbed into their Ford Convertibles, Morris Minors, Baby Austins or flashy Packards and Daimlers.

But of course Dehra in the 'fifties' was a town of bicycles. Students, shopkeepers, Army cadets, office workers, all used them. The scooter (or Lambretta) had only just been invented, and it would be several years before it took over from the bicycle. It was still unaffordable for the great majority.

I was awkward on a bicycle and frequently fell off, breaking my arm on one occasion. But this did not prevent me from joining my friends on cycle rides to the Sulphur springs, or to Premnagar (where the Military Academy was situated) or along the Hardwar road and down to the riverbed at Lachiwala.

In Jersey, I found an old cycle belonging to my cousin, and I rode from St. Helier where we lived, to St Brelade's Bay, at the other end of the island. But returning after dark, I was hauled up for riding without lights. I had no idea that cycles had also to be equipped with lights. Back in Dehra, we never used them!

The attic room had no view, so one of my favourite occupations, gazing out of windows, came to a stop. But perhaps this was helpful in that it made me concentrate on the sheet of paper in my typewriter. After about six months, I had a book of sorts ready for submission to any publisher who was prepared to look at it. Meanwhile, I had been through at least three jobs and had even been offered a post in the Jersey Civil Service, having successfully taken the local civil service exam—something I had done out of sheer boredom, as I had no intention of settling permanently on the island.

I had been keeping a diary of sorts and in some of the entries I had expressed my desire to get back to India, and my discontent at having to stay with relatives who were unsympathetic, not only to my feelings for India but also to my ambitions to become a writer. The diary fell into my uncle's hands. He read it, and was naturally upset. We had a row. I was contrite; but a few days later I packed my suitcases (all two of them) and stepped on to the ferry that was to take me to Southampton and then to London. Lesson One: Don't leave your personal diaries lying around!

But perhaps it was all for the best, otherwise I might have hung around in Jersey for another year or two, to the detriment of my personal happiness and my writing ambitions.

I arrived in London in the middle of a thick yellow November fog—those were the days of the killer London fogs—and after a search found the Students' Hostel where I was given a cubicle to myself. But I did not stay there very long; the available food was awful. As soon as I got an office job—not too difficult in the 1950s—I rented an attic room in Belsize Park, the first of many bedsitters that I was to live in during my three-year sojourn in London.

From Belsize Park I was to move to Haverstock Hill (close to Hampstead Heath), then to South London for a short time, and finally to Swiss Cottage. Most of my landladies were Jewish—refugees from persecution in pre-war Europe—and I too was a refugee of sorts, still very unsure of where I belonged. Was it England, the land of my father, or India, the land of my birth? But my father had also been born in India, had grown up and made a living there, visiting his father's land, England, only a couple of times during his life.

The link with Britain was tenuous, based on heredity rather than upbringing. It was more in the mind. It was a literary England I had been drawn to, not a physical England. And in fact, I took several exploratory walks around 'literary' London, visiting houses or streets where famous writers had once lived; in particular the East End and dockland, for I had grown up on the novels and stories of Dickens, Smollett, Captain Marryat, and W.W. Jacobs. But I did not make many English friends. If they were a reserved race, I was even more reserved. Always shy, I waited for others to take the initiative. In India, people will take the initiative, they lose no time in getting to know you. Not so in England. They were too polite to look at you. And in that respect, I was more English than the English.

The gentleman who lived on the floor below me occasionally went so far as to greet me with the observation, 'Beastly weather, isn't it?'

And I would respond by saying, 'Oh, perfectly beastly,' and pass on.

How different it was when I bumped into a Gujarati boy, Praveen, who lived on the basement floor. He gave me a winning smile, and I remember saying, 'Oh, to be in Bombay now that winter's here,' and immediately we were friends.

He was only seventeen, a year or two younger than me, and he was studying at one of the polytechnics with a view to getting into the London School of Economics. At that time, most of the Indians in London were students, the great immigration rush was still a long way off,, and racial antagonisms were directed more at the recently arrived West Indians than at Asians.

Praveen took me on the rounds of the coffee bars, then proliferating all over London, and introduced me to other students, among them a Vietnamese, called Thanh, who cultivated my friendship because, as he said, 'I want to speak English.' When he discovered that my accent was very un-English (you could have called it Welsh with an Anglo-Indian interaction), he dropped me like a hot brick. He was very frank, he was not interested in friendship, he said, only in improving his accent. I heard later that he'd attached himself to a young journalist from up north, who spoke broad Yorkshire.

Most evenings I remained in my room and worked on my novel. From being a journal it had become a first person narrative, and now I was turning it into fiction in the third person. The title had also undergone a few changes, but finally I settled on *The Room on the Roof*.

Into it I put all the love and affection I felt for the friends I had left behind in Dehra. It was more than nostalgia, it was a recreation of the people, places and incidents of that last year in India. I did not want it to fade away. The riverbanks at Hardwar, the mango-groves of the Doon, the poinsettias and bougainvillaea, the games on the parade ground, the chaat shops near the Clock Tower, the summer heat, the monsoon downpours, romping naked in the rain, sitting on railway platforms, gnawing at a stick of sugar cane, listening to street cries.... All this and more came crowding upon me as I sat writing before the gas fire in my little room.

When it grew very cold, I used an old overcoat given to me by Diana Athill, the junior partner at Andre Deutsch, who had promised to publish *The Room* if I rewrote it as a novel. Another who encouraged me was a BBC producer, Prudence Smith, who got me to give a couple of Talks on Radio's Third Programme. I felt I was getting somewhere; and when I found myself confined to the Hampstead General Hospital for almost a month, with a mysterious disease which had affected the vision in my right eye, I used the left to catch up on my reading and to write a couple of short stories.

A nurse brought a tray of books around the ward every afternoon, and thanks to this courtesy, I was able to discover the delightful stories of William Saroyan, and Denton Welch's sensitive first novel *Maiden Voyage*. Saroyan, a Pulitzer Prize winner for his play *The Time of Your Life,* was then very successful and popular. Denton's promising career had been cut short by a terrible accident. Out cycling on a country road, he had been knocked down by a speeding motorist. He had lived for several years, smuggling against crippling injuries and almost completing his sensitive autobiography *A Voice in the Clouds*. He was thirty-one when he died. Towards the end, he could only work for three or four minutes at a time. Complications set in, and the left side of his heart started failing. Even then, he made a terrific effort to finish his book. His friend Eric wrote—'Denton was upheld by the high courage which seemed somehow the fruit of his rare intelligence.'

The work of these writers, together with the bottle of Guinness I was given every day as a tonic (they had found me somewhat undernourished), meant that I walked out of the hospital with a spring in my step and a determination to succeed.

But Andre Deutsch was still dithering over my book. The firm was doing well, but he didn't like taking risks. No publisher likes losing money. And he wasn't going to make much out of my novel, a subjective and unsensational work.

But I resented his indecision. So I returned the small amount he'd paid me byway of an option, and demanded the return of my manuscript. Back came an apologetic letter and an advance (then £50) against publication.

Today, almost fifty years later, the firm of Andre Deutsch has gone, but *The Room on the Roof* is still in print, still making friends. This is not something that I gloat over, it only goes to show that books are unpredictable commodities, and that the most successful authors and publishers often fall by the wayside. Publishers go out of business, writers fade from the public mind. Even Saroyan is forgotten now. I'll be forgotten too, some day.

There were to be further delays before *The Room* was published, and I was back in India when it did come out. By then I'd almost forgotten about the book! But it picked up the John Llewellyn Rhys Prize, an award that also went to V.S. Naipaul a year later, for his first book. It was then worth only £50. There were no big sponsors in those days. It is now sponsored by a British newspaper and is worth £5,000. This was turned down last year by another Indian writer, who disagreed with the paper's policies.

Meanwhile, in London, there were other distractions. I loved stage musicals, and if I had a little money to spare I went to the theatre, taking in such productions as *Porgy and Bess*, *Paint Your Wagon*, *Pal Joey*, *Teahouse of the August Moon*, and the occasional review. And of course the annual presentation of *Peter Pan* at the Scala theatre, not far from where I worked. I had grown up on *Peter Pan*, first read to me by my father in distant Jamnagar, and at school I had read Barrie's other plays and been charmed by them; but, like operetta, they had gone out of fashion and only the ageless Peter remained. 'Do you believe in fairies?' he asks in the play. And to save Tinker Bell from extinction, I clapped with the rest of the audience. But did I really believe in fairies? I looked for them in Kensington Gardens, where Peter Pan's statue stood, and found a few mothers pushing their perambulators, but no fairies. And I looked in Hyde Park, but found only courting couples. And I looked all over Leicester Square, but instead of fairies I found prostitutes soliciting business. As I was still looking for romance, I crept back to my room and my portable typewriter—I would have to create my own romance.

The small portable had been in the windows of a Jersey department store, and every time I passed the store, I glanced at the window to see if the typewriter was still there. It seemed to be waiting for me to come in and take it away. I longed to buy it, partly because I had to type out the final drafts of my book, and also because it looked very dainty and attractive. It was definitely out to seduce me. Finally, with the help of a loan from Mr Bromley, a kindly senior clerk, I bought the machine. It cost only £12, but that was three month's wages at the time. It accompanied me to London, and then a couple of years later to India, giving me good service in Dehradun, New Delhi, and then Mussoorie where it finally succumbed to the damp monsoon climate.

My worldly possessions had increased, not only by the typewriter, but also by a record player which I had bought second hand from a Thai student. I had become an ardent fan of the black singer, Eartha Kitt, and had bought all her records; but they were no good without a player until the Thai boy came to my rescue. Then the sensual, throaty voice of Eartha reverberated through the lodging house, bringing complaints from the landlady and the gentleman downstairs. I had to keep the volume low, which wasn't much fun.

I was also fond of the clarinet *(turj)* playing of an Indian musician, Master Ibrahim, and I had some of his recordings which transported me back to the streets and bazaars of small-town India. Light, lilting and tuneful, I preferred this sort of flute music to the warblings of the more popular songsters.

Praveen liked gangster films and wanted me to accompany him to anything which featured Humphrey Bogart, James Cagney, George Raft and other tough guys. Praveen wanted to be a tough guy himself and often struck a Bogart-like pose, cigarette dangling from the side of his mouth. There was nothing tough about Praveen, who was really rather delicate, but his affectations were charming and risible.

One day he announced that he was returning to India for a few months, as his ailing mother was anxious to see him. He asked me to come along too, to give him company during the three-week voyage. To do so, I would have to throw up my job, but I had already thrown up several jobs. They were simply stopgaps until I could establish myself as a writer. I hadn't the slightest intention or ambition of being a senior clerk or even an executive for the firm in which I was working. The only problem in leaving England then was that I would have to leave my book in limbo, as there was still no guarantee that Deutsch would publish it. But it was time I went on to write other things; time to strike out on my own, to take a chance with India. The ships were full of British and Anglo-Indian families coming to England, to make a 'better future' for themselves. I would do the opposite, go into reverse, and make my future, for good or ill, in the land of my birth.

My passport was in order, and I had only to give a week's notice to my employers. I had saved up about £200, and of this £50 went on the cost of my passage, London to Bombay. Praveen and I boarded the S.S. Batory, a Polish liner with a reputation for running into trouble. We had no difficulty in securing berths in tourist class. Praveen had every intention of returning to England to complete his studies. My own intentions were very vague. I knew there would be no job for me in India, but I was quietly confident that I could make a living from writing, and that too in the English language.

The Batory lived up to its reputation. Some of the crew went missing at Gibraltar. A passenger fell overboard in the Red Sea. Lifeboats were lowered, but he could not be found.

Praveen fell in love with an Egyptian girl who disembarked

at Aden. He followed her ashore, and I had to run after him and get him back to the ship. As we docked at Ballard Pier, a fire broke out in one of the holds, but by then we were safely ashore. Praveen was swamped by relatives who carried him off to the suburbs of Bombay. I made my way to Victoria Terminus and boarded the Dehradun Express.

It was a slow passenger train, which went chugging through several states in the general direction of northern India. Two days and two nights later we crawled through the eastern Doon. It was early March. The mango trees were in blossom, the peacocks were calling, and Belsize Park was far away.

Ten

Friends of My Youth

1
SUDHEER

FRIENDSHIP IS ALL ABOUT DOING THINGS together. It may be climbing a mountain, fishing in a mountain stream, cycling along a country road, camping in a forest clearing, or simply travelling together and sharing the experiences that a new place can bring.

On at least two of these counts, Sudheer qualified as a friend, albeit a troublesome one, given to involving me in his adolescent escapades.

I met him in Dehra soon after my return from England. He turned up at my room, saying he'd heard I was a writer and did I have any comics to lend him?

'I don't write comics,' I said; but there were some comics lying around, left over from my own boyhood collection, so I gave these to the lanky youth who stood smiling in the doorway, and he thanked me and said he'd bring them back. From my window I saw him cycling off in the general direction of Dalanwala.

He turned up again a few days later and dumped a large pile of new-looking comics on my desk. 'Here are all the latest,' he announced. 'You can keep them for me. I'm not allowed to read comics at home.'

It was only weeks later that I learnt he was given to pilfering comics and magazines from the town's bookstores. In no time at all, I'd become a receiver of stolen goods!

My landlady had warned me against Sudheer and so had one or two others. He had acquired a certain notoriety for having been expelled from his school. He had been in charge of the library, and before a consignment of newly-acquired books could be registered and library stamped, he had sold them back to the bookshop from which they had originally been purchased. Very enterprising but not to be countenanced in a very pukka public school. He was now studying in a municipal school, too poor to afford a library.

Sudheer was an amoral scamp all right, but I found it difficult to avoid him, or to resist his undeniable and openly affectionate manner. He could make you laugh. And anyone who can do that is easily forgiven for a great many faults.

One day he produced a couple of white mice from his pockets and left them on my desk.

'You keep them for me,' he said. 'I'm not allowed to keep them at home.'

There were a great many things he was not allowed to keep at home. Anyway, the white mice were given a home in an old cupboard, where my landlady kept unwanted dishes, pots and pans, and they were quite happy there, being fed on bits of bread or chapati, until one day I heard shrieks from the storeroom, and charging into it, found my dear stout landlady having hysterics as one of the white mice sought refuge under her blouse and the other ran frantically up and down her back.

Sudheer had to find another home for the white mice. It was that, or finding another home for myself.

Most young men, boys, and quite a few girls used bicycles. There was a cycle-hire shop across the road, and Sudheer persuaded me to hire cycles for both of us. We cycled out of town, through tea gardens and mustard fields, and down a forest road until we discovered a small, shallow river where we bathed and wrestled on the sand. Although I was three or four years older than Sudheer, he was much the stronger, being about six-foot tall and broad in the shoulders. His parents had come from Bhanu, a rough and ready district on the North West Frontier, as a result of the partition of the country. His father ran a small press situated behind the Sabzi Mandi and brought out a weekly newspaper called *The Frontier Times*.

We came to the stream quite often. It was Sudheer's way

of playing truant from school without being detected in the bazaar or at the cinema. He was sixteen when I met him, and eighteen when we parted, but I can't recall that he ever showed any interest in his schoolwork.

He took me to his home in the Karanpur bazaar, then a stronghold of the Bhanu community. The Karanpur boys were an aggressive lot and resented Sudheer's friendship with an angrez. To avoid a confrontation, I would use the back alleys and side streets to get to and from the house in which they lived.

Sudheer had been overindulged by his mother, who protected him from his father's wrath. Both parents felt I might have an 'improving' influence on their son, and encouraged our friendship. His elder sister seemed more doubtful. She felt he was incorrigible, beyond redemption, and that I was not much better, and she was probably right.

The father invited me to his small press and asked me if I'd like to work with him. I agreed to help with the newspaper for a couple of hours every morning. This involved proofreading and editing news agency reports. Uninspiring work, but useful.

Meanwhile, Sudheer had got hold of a pet monkey, and he carried it about in the basket attached to the handlebar of his bicycle. He used it to ingratiate himself with the girls. 'How sweet! How pretty!' they would exclaim, and Sudheer would get the monkey to show them its tricks.

After some time, however, the monkey appeared to be infected by Sudheer's amorous nature, and would make obscene gestures which were not appreciated by his former admirers. On one occasion, the monkey made off with a girl's dupatta. A chase ensued, and the dupatta retrieved, but the outcome of it all was that Sudheer was accosted by the girl's brothers and given a black eye and a bruised cheek. His father took the monkey away and returned it to the itinerant juggler who had sold it to the young man.

Sudheer soon developed an insatiable need for money. He wasn't getting anything at home, apart from what he pinched from his mother and sister, and his father urged me not to give the boy any money. After paying for my boarding and lodging I had very little to spare, but Sudheer seemed to sense when a money order or cheque arrived, and would hang around, spinning tall tales of great financial distress until, in order to be rid of him, I would give him five to ten rupees. (In those days, a magazine payment seldom exceeded fifty rupees.)

He was becoming something of a trial, constantly interrupting me in my work, and even picking up confectionery from my landlady's small shop and charging it to my account. I had stopped going for bicycle rides. He had wrecked one of the cycles and the shopkeeper held me responsible for repairs.

The sad thing was that Sudheer had no other friends. He did not go in for team games or for music or other creative pursuits which might have helped him to move around with people of his own age group. He was a loner with a propensity for mischief. Had he entered a bicycle race, he would have won easily. Forever eluding a variety of pursuers, he was extremely fast on his bike. But we did not have cycle races in Dehra.

And then, for a blessed two or three weeks, I saw nothing of my unpredictable friend.

I discovered later, that he had taken a fancy to a young schoolteacher, about five years his senior, who lived in a hostel up at Rajpur. His cycle rides took him in that direction. As usual, his charm proved irresistible, and it wasn't long before the teacher and the acolyte were taking rides together down lonely forest roads. This was all right by me, of course, but it wasn't the norm with the middle class matrons of small town India, at least not in 1957. Hostel wardens, other students, and naturally Sudheer's parents, were all in a state of agitation. So I wasn't surprised when Sudheer turned up in my room to announce that he was on his way to Nahan, to study at an inter-college there.

Nahan was a small hill town about sixty miles from Dehra. Sudheer was banished to the home of his mama, an uncle who was a subinspector in the local police force. He had promised to see that Sudheer stayed out of trouble.

Whether he succeeded or not, I could not tell, for a couple of months later I gave up my rooms in Dehra and left for Delhi. I lost touch with Sudheer's family, and it was only several years later, when I bumped into an old acquaintance, that I was given news of my erstwhile friend.

He had apparently done quite well for himself. Taking off for Calcutta, he had used his charm and his fluent English to land a job as an assistant on a tea-estate. Here he had proved quite efficient, earning the approval of his manager and employers. But his roving eyes soon got him into trouble. The women working in the tea gardens became prey to his amorous and amoral nature. Keeping one mistress was acceptable. Keeping several was asking for trouble. He was found dead, early one morning with his throat cut.

2

THE ROYAL CAFÈ SET

Dehra was going through a slump in those days, and there wasn't much work for anyone—least of all for my neighbour, Suresh Mathur, an Income Tax lawyer, who was broke for two reasons. To begin with, there was not much work going around, as those with taxable incomes were few and far between. Apart from that, when he did get work, he was slow and half-hearted about getting it done. This was because he seldom got up before eleven in the morning, and by the time he took a bus down from Rajpur and reached his own small office (next door to my rooms), or the Income Tax office a little further on, it was lunchtime and all the tax officials were out. Suresh would then repair to the Royal Cafè for a beer or two (often at my expense) and this would stretch into a gin and tonic, after which he would stagger up to his first floor office and collapse on the sofa for an afternoon nap. He would wake up at six, after the Income Tax office had closed.

I occupied two rooms next to his office, and we were on friendly terms, sharing an enthusiasm for the humorous works of P.G. Wodehouse. I think he modelled himself on Bertie Wooster for he would often turn up wearing mauve or yellow socks or a pink shirt and a bright green tie—enough to make anyone in his company feel quite liverish. Unlike Bertie Wooster, he did not have a Jeeves to look after him and get him out of various scrapes. I tried not to be too friendly, as Suresh was in the habit of borrowing lavishly from all his friends, conveniently forgetting to return the amounts. I wasn't well off and could ill afford the company of a spendthrift friend. Sudheer was trouble enough.

Dehra, in those days, was full of people living on borrowed money or no money at all. Hence, the large number of disconnected telephone and electric lines. I did not have electricity myself, simply because the previous tenant had taken off, leaving me with outstandings of over a thousand rupees, then a princely sum. My monthly income seldom exceeded five hundred rupees. No matter. There was plenty of kerosene available, and the oil lamp lent a romantic glow to my literary endeavours.

Looking back, I am amazed at the number of people who were quite broke. There was William Matheson, a Swiss journalist, whose remittances from Zurich never seemed to turn up; my landlady, whose husband had deserted her two years previously; Mr Madan, who dealt in second-hand cars which no one wanted; the owner of the corner restaurant, who sat in solitary splendour surrounded by empty tables; and the proprietor of the Ideal Book Depot, who was selling off his stock of unsold books and becoming a departmental store. We complain that few people buy or read books today, but I can assure you that there were even fewer customers in the fifties and sixties. Only doctors, dentists, and the proprietors of English schools were making money.

Suresh spent whatever cash came his way, and borrowed more. He had an advantage over the rest of us—he owned an old bungalow, inherited from his father, up at Rajpur in the foothills, where he lived alone with an old manservant. And owning a property gave him some standing with his creditors. The grounds boasted of a mango and lichi orchard, and these he gave out on contract every year, so that his friends did not even get to enjoy some of his produce. The proceeds helped him to pay his office rent in town, with a little left over to give small amounts on account to the owner of the Royal Cafè.

If a lawyer could be hard up, what chance had a journalist? And yet, William Matheson had everything going for him from the start, when he came out to India as an assistant to Von Hesseltein, correspondent for some of the German papers. Von Hesseltein passed on some of the assignments to William, and for a time, all went well. William lived with Von Hesseltein and his family, and was also friendly with Suresh, often paying for the drinks at the Royal Cafè. Then

William committed the folly (if not the sin) of having an affair with Von Hesseltein's wife. Von Hesseltein was not the understanding sort. He threw William out of the house and stopped giving him work.

William hired an old typewriter and set himself up as a correspondent in his own right, living and working from a room in the Doon Guest House. At first he was welcome there, having paid a three-month advance for room and board. He bombarded the Swiss and German papers with his articles, but there were very few takers. No one in Europe was really interested in India's five-year plans, or Corbusier's Chandigarh, or the Bhakra-Nangal Dam. Book publishing in India was confined to textbooks, otherwise William might have published a vivid account of his experiences in the French Foreign Legion. After two or three rums at the Royal Cafè, he would regale us with tales of his exploits in the Legion, before and after the siege of Dien Bien-Phu. Some of his stories had the ring of truth, others (particularly his sexual exploits) were obviously tall tales; but I was happy to pay for the beer or coffee in order to hear him spin them out.

Those were glorious days for an unknown freelance writer. I was realizing my dream of living by my pen, and I was doing it from a small town in north India, having turned my back on both London and New Delhi. I had no ambitions to be a great writer, or even a famous one, or even a rich one. All I wanted to do was write. And I wanted a few readers and the occasional cheque so I could carry on living my dream.

The cheques came along in their own desultory way—fifty rupees from the *Weekly*, or thirty-five from *The Statesman* or the same from *Sport* and *Pastime*, and so on—just enough to get by, and to be the envy of Suresh Mathur, William Matheson, and a few others, professional people who felt that I had no business earning more then they did. Suresh even declared that I should have been paying tax, and offered to represent me, his other clients having gone elsewhere.

And there was old Colonel Wilkie, living on a small pension in a corner room of the White House Hotel. His wife had left him some years before, presumably because of his drinking, but he claimed to have left her because of her obsession with moving the furniture—it seems she was always shifting things about, changing rooms, throwing out perfectly sound tables and chairs and replacing them with fancy stuff picked up here and there. If he took a liking to a particular easy chair and showed signs of setting down in it, it would disappear the next day to be replaced by something horribly ugly and uncomfortable.

'It was a form of mental torture,' said Colonel Wilkie, confiding in me over a glass of beer on the White House verandah. 'The sitting room was cluttered with all sorts of ornamental junk and flimsy side tables, so that I was constantly falling over the damn things. It was like a minefield! And the mines were never in the same place. You've noticed that I walk with a limp?'

'First World War?' I ventured. 'Wounded at Ypres? Or was it Flanders?'

'Nothing of the sort,' snorted the colonel. 'I did get one or two flesh wounds but they were nothing as compared to the damage inflicted on me by those damned shifting tables and chairs. Fell over a coffee table and dislocated my shoulder. Then broke an ankle negotiating a stool that was in the wrong place. Bookshelf fell on me. Tripped on a rolled up carpet. Hit by a curtain rod. Would you have put up with it?' 'No,' I had to admit.

'Had to leave her, of course. She went off to England. Send her an allowance. Half my pension! All spent on furniture!'

'It's a superstition of sorts, I suppose. Collecting things.'

The colonel told me that the final straw was when his favourite spring bed had suddenly been replaced by a bed made up of hard wooden slats. It was sheer torture trying to sleep on it, and he had left his house and moved into the White House Hotel as a permanent guest.

Now he couldn't allow anyone to touch or tidy up anything in his room. There were beer stains on the tablecloth, cobwebs on his family pictures, dust on his books, empty medicine bottles on his dressing table, and mice nesting in his old, discarded boots. He had gone to the other extreme and wouldn't have anything changed or moved in his room.

I didn't see much of the room because we usually sat out on the verandah, waited upon by one of the hotel bearers, who came over with bottles of beer that I dutifully paid for, the colonel having exhausted his credit. I suppose he was in his late sixties then. He never went anywhere, not even for a walk in the compound. He blamed this inactivity on his gout, but it was really inertia and an unwillingness to leave the precincts of the bar, where he could cadge the occasional drink from a sympathetic guest. I am that age now, and not half as active as I used to be, but there are people to live for, and tales to tell, and I keep writing. It is important to keep writing.

Colonel Wilkie had given up on life. I suppose he could have gone off to England, but he would have been more miserable there, with no one to buy him a drink (since he wasn't likely to reciprocate), and the possibility of his wife turning up again to rearrange the furniture.

3
'BIBIJI'

My landlady was a remarkable woman, and this little memoir of Dehra in the 1950s would be incomplete without a sketch of hers.

She would often say, 'Ruskin, one day you must write my life story,' and I would promise to do so. And although she really deserves a book to herself, I shall try to do justice to her in these few pages.

She was, in fact, my Punjabi stepfather's first wife. Does

that sound confusing? It was certainly complicated. And you might well ask, why on earth were you living with your stepfather's first wife instead of your stepfather and mother?

The answer is simple. I got on rather well with this rotund, well-built lady, and sympathized with her predicament. She had been married at a young age to my stepfather, who was something of a playboy, and who ran the photographic saloon he had received as part of her dowry. When he left her for my mother, he sold the saloon and gave his first wife part of the premises. In order to sustain herself and two small children, she started a small provision store and thus became Dehra's first lady shopkeeper.

I had just started freelancing from Dehra and was not keen on joining my mother and stepfather in Delhi. When 'Bibiji'—as I called her—offered me a portion of her flat on very reasonable terms, I accepted without hesitation and was to spend the next two years above her little shop on Rajpur Road. Almost fifty years later, the flat in still there, but it is now an ice cream parlour! Poetic justice, perhaps.

'Bibiji' sold the usual provisions. Occasionally, I lent a helping hand and soon learnt the names of the various lentils arrayed before us—*moong, malka, masoor, arhar, channa, rajma,* etc. She bought her rice, flour, and other items wholesale from the *mandi,* and sometimes I would accompany her on an early morning march to the *mandi* (about two miles distant) where we would load a handcart with her purchases. She was immensely strong and could lift sacks of wheat or rice that left me gasping. I can't say I blame my rather skinny stepfather for staying out of her reach.

She had a helper, a Bihari youth, who would trundle the cart back to the shop and help with the loading and unloading. Before opening the shop (at around 8 a.m.) she would make our breakfast—parathas with my favourite *shalgam* pickle, and in winter, a delicious *kanji* made from the juice of red carrots. When the shop opened, I would go upstairs to do my writing while she conducted the day's business.

Sometimes she would ask me to help her with her accounts, or in making out a bill, for she was barely literate. But she was an astute shopkeeper; she knew instinctively, who was good for credit and who was strictly *nakad* (cash). She would also warn me against friends who borrowed money without any intention of returning it; warnings that I failed to heed. Friends in perpetual need there were aplenty—Sudheer, William, Suresh and a couple of others—and I am amazed that I didn't have to borrow too, considering the uncertain nature of my income. Those little cheques and money orders from magazines did not always arrive in time. But sooner or later something did turn up. I was very lucky.

Bibiji had a friend, a neighbour, Mrs Singh, an attractive woman in her thirties who smoked a hookah and regaled us with tales of ghosts and *chudails* from her village near Agra. We did not see much of her husband who was an excise inspector. He was busy making money.

Bibiji and Mrs Singh were almost inseparable, which was quite understandable in view of the fact that both had absentee husbands. They were really happy together. During the day Mrs. Singh would sit in the shop, observing the customers. And afterwards she would entertain us to clever imitations of the more odd or eccentric among them. At night, after the shop was closed, Bibiji and her friend would make themselves comfortable on the same cot (creaking beneath their combined weights), wrap themselves in a razai or blanket and invite me to sit on the next *charpai* and listen to their yarns or tell them a few of my own. Mrs. Singh had a small son, not very bright, who was continually eating laddoos, jalebis, barfis and other sweets. Quite appropriately, he was called Laddoo. And I believe, he grew into one.

Bibiji's son and daughter were then at a residential school. They came home occasionally. So did Mr Singh, with more sweets for his son. He did not appear to find anything unusual in his wife's intimate relationship with Bibiji. His mind was obviously on other things.

Bibiji and Mrs. Singh both made plans to get me married. When I protested, saying I was only twenty-three, they said I was old enough. Bibiji had an eye on an Anglo-Indian schoolteacher who sometimes came to the shop, but Mrs Singh turned her down, saying she had very spindly legs. Instead, she suggested the daughter of the local padre, a glamourous-looking, dusky beauty, but Bibiji vetoed the proposal, saying the young lady used too much make-up and already displayed too much fat around the waistline. Both agreed that I should marry a plain-looking girl who could cook, use a sewing machine, and speak a little English.

'And be strong in the legs,' I added, much to Mrs Singh's approval.

They did not know it, but I was enamoured of Kamla, a girl from the hills, who lived with her parents in quarters behind the flat. She was always giving me mischievous glances with her dark, beautiful, expressive eyes. And whenever I passed her on the landing, we exchanged pleasantries and friendly banter; it was as though we had known each other for a long time. But she was already betrothed, and that too to a much older man, a widower, who owned some land outside the town. Kamla's family was poor, her father was in debt, and it was to be a marriage of convenience. There was nothing much I could do about it—landless, and without prospects— but after the marriage had taken place and she had left for her new home, I befriended her younger brother and through him sent her my good wishes from time to time. She is just a distant memory now, but a bright one, like a forget-me-not blooming on a bare rock. Would I have married her, had I been able to? She was simple, unlettered; but I might have taken the chance.

Those two years on Rajpur Road were an eventful time, what with the visitations of Sudheer, the company of William and Suresh, the participation in Bibiji's little shop, the evanescent friendship with Kamla. I did a lot of writing and even sold a few stories here and there; but the returns were modest, barely adequate. Everyone was urging me to try my luck in Delhi. And so I bid goodbye to sleepy little Dehra (as it then was) and took a bus to the capital. I did no better there as a writer, but I found a job of sorts and that kept me going for a couple of years.

But to return to Bibiji, I cannot just leave her in limbo. She continued to run her shop for several years, and it was only failing health that forced her to close it. She sold the business and went to live with her married daughter in New Delhi. I saw her from time to time. In spite of high blood pressure, diabetes, and eventually blindness, she lived on into her eighties. She was always glad to see me, and never gave up trying to find a suitable bride for me.

The last time I saw her, shortly before she died, she said, 'Ruskin, there is this widow—lady who lives down the road and comes over sometimes. She has two children but they are grown up. She feels lonely in her big house. If you like, I'll talk to her. Its time you settled down. And she's only sixty.'

'Thanks, Bibiji,' I said, holding both ears. 'But I think I'll settle down in my next life.'

Eleven

Midwinter, Deserted Hill Station

I see you every day
Walk barefoot on the frozen ground.
I want to be your friend,
But you look the other way.

I see you every day
Go hungry in the bitter cold;
I'd gladly share my food,
But you look the other way.

I hear you every night
Cough desolately in the dark;
I'd share my warmth with you,
But you look the other way.

I see you every day
Pass lonely on my lonely way.
I'd gladly walk with you;
But you turn away.

Twelve

Adventures in Reading

1
BEAUTY IN SMALL BOOKS

You DON'T SEE THEM SO OFTEN NOW, THOSE tiny books and almanacs—genuine pocketbooks—once so popular with our parents and grandparents; much smaller than the average paperback, often smaller than the palm of the hand. With the advent of coffee-table books, new books keep growing bigger and bigger, rivalling tombstones! And one day, like Alice after drinking from the wrong bottle, they will reach the ceiling and won't have anywhere else to go. The average publisher, who apparently believes that large profits are linked to large books, must look upon these old miniatures with amusement or scorn. They were not meant for a coffee table, true. They were meant for true book-lovers and readers, for they took up very little space—you could slip them into your pocket without any discomfort, either to you or to the pocket.

I have a small collection of these little books, treasured over the years. Foremost is my father's prayer book and psalter, with his name, 'Aubrey Bond, Lovedale, 1917', inscribed on the inside back cover. Lovedale is a school in the Nilgiri Hills in south India, where, as a young man, he did his teacher's training. He gave it to me soon after I went to a boarding school in Shimla in 1944, and my own name is inscribed on it in his beautiful handwriting.

Another beautiful little prayer book in my collection is called *The Finger Prayer Book*. Bound in soft leather, it is about the same length and breadth as the average middle finger. Replete with psalms, it is the complete book of common prayer and not an abridgement; a marvel of miniature book production.

Not much larger is a delicate item in calf-leather, *The Humour of Charles Lamb*. It fits into my wallet and often stays there. It has a tiny portrait of the great essayist, followed by some thirty to forty extracts from his essays, such as this favourite of mine: 'Every dead man must take upon himself to be lecturing me with his odious truism, that "Such as he is now, I must shortly be". Not so shortly friend, perhaps as thou imaginest. In the meantime, I am alive. I move about. I am worth twenty of thee. Know thy betters!'

No fatalist, Lamb. He made no compromise with Father Time. He affirmed that in age we must be as glowing and tempestuous as in youth! And yet Lamb is thought to be an old-fashioned writer.

Another favourite among my 'little' books is *The Pocket Trivet, An Anthology for Optimists*, published by *The Morning Post* newspaper in 1932. But what is a trivet? The unenlightened may well ask. Well, it's a stand for a small pot or kettle, fixed securely over a grate. To be right as a trivet is to be perfectly right. Just right, like the short sayings in this book, which is further enlivened by a number of charming woodcuts based on the seventeenth centuiy originals; such as the illustration of a moth hovering over a candle flame and below it the legend—'I seeke mine owne hurt.'

But the sayings are mostly of a cheering nature, such as Emerson's 'Hitch your wagon to a star!' or the West Indian proverb: 'Every day no Christmas, an' every day no rainy day.'

My book of trivets is a happy example of much concentrated wisdom being collected in a small space—the beauty separated from the dross. It helps me to forget the dilapidated building in which I live and to look instead, at the ever-changing cloud patterns as seen from my bedroom windows. There is no end to the shapes made by the clouds, or to the stories they set off in my head. We don't have to circle the world in order to find beauty and fulfilment. After all, most of living has to happen in the mind. And, to quote one anonymous sage from my trivet, 'The world is only the size of each man's head.'

2
WRITTEN BY HAND

Amongst the current fraternity of writers, I must be that very rare person—an author who actually writes by hand!

Soon after the invention of the typewriter, most editors and publishers understandably refused to look at any manscript that was handwritten. A decade or two earlier, when Dickens and Balzac had submitted their hefty manuscrips in longhand, no one had raised any objection. Had their handwriting been awful, their manuscripts would still have been read. Fortunately for all concerned, most writers, famous or obscure, took pains over their handwriting. For some, it was an art in itself, and many of those early manuscripts are a pleasure to look at and read.

And it wasn't only authors who wrote with an elegant hand. Parents and grandparents of most of us had distinctive styles of their own. I still have my father's last letter, written to me when I was at boarding school in Shimla some fifty years ago. He used large, beautifully formed letters, and his thoughts seemed to have the same flow and clarity as his handwriting.

In his letter he advises me (then a nine-year-old) about my own handwriting; 'I wanted to write before about your writing. Ruskin...sometimes I get letters from you in very small writing, as if you wanted to squeeze everything into one sheet of letter paper. It is not good for you or for your eyes, to get into the habit of writing too small... Try and form a larger style of handwriting—use more paper if necessary!'

I did my best to follow his advice, and I'm glad to report that after nearly forty years of the writing life, most people can still read my handwriting!

Word processors are all the rage now, and I have no objection to these mechanical aids any more than I have to my old Olympia typewriter, made in 1956 and still going strong. Although I do all my writing in longhand, I follow the conventions by typing a second draft. But I would not enjoy my writing if I had to do it straight on to a machine. It isn't just the pleasure of writing longhand. I like taking my notebooks and writing pads to odd places. This particular essay is being written on the steps of my small cottage facing Pari Tibba (Fairy Hill). Part of the reason for sitting here is that there is a new postman on this route, and I don't want him to miss me.

For a freelance writer, the postman is almost as important as a publisher. I could, of course, sit here doing nothing, but as I have pencil and paper with me, and feel like using them, I shall write until the postman comes and maybe after he has gone, too! There is really no way in which I could set up a word-processor on these steps.

There are a number of favourite places where I do my writing. One is under the chestnut tree on the slope above the cottage. Word processors were not designed keeping mountain slopes in mind. But armed with a pen (or pencil) and paper, I can lie on the grass and write for hours. On one occasion, last month, I did take my typewriter into the garden, and I am still trying to extricate an acorn from under the keys, while the roller seems permanently stained yellow with some fine pollen-dust from the deodar trees.

My friends keep telling me about all the wonderful things I can do with a word processor, but they haven't got around to finding me one that I can take to bed, for that is another place where I do much of my writing—especially on cold winter nights, when it is impossible to keep the cottage warm.

While the wind howls outside, and snow piles up on the windowsill, I am warm under my quilt, writing pad on my knees, ballpoint pen at the ready And if, next day, the weather is warm and sunny, these simple aids will accompany me on a long walk, ready for instant use should I wish to record an incident, a prospect, a conversation, or simply a train of thought.

When I think of the great eighteenth-and nineteenth-century writers, scratching away with their quill pens, filling hundreds of pages every month, I am amazed to find that their handwriting did not deteriorate into the sort of hieroglyphics that often make up the average doctor's prescription today. They knew they had to write legibly, if only for the sake of the typesetters.

Both Dickens and Thackeray had good, clear, flourishing styles. (Thackeray was a clever illustrator, too.) Somerset Maugham had an upright, legible hand. Churchill's neat handwriting never wavered, even when he was under stress.

I like the bold, clear, straightforward hand of Abraham Lincoln; it mirrors the man. Mahatma Gandhi, another great soul who fell to the assassin's bullet, had many similarities of both handwriting and outlook.

Not everyone had a beautiful hand. King Henry VIII had an untidy scrawl, but then, he was not a man of much refinement. Guy Fawkes, who tried to blow up the British Parliament, had a very shaky hand. With such a quiver, no wonder he failed in his attempt! Hitler's signature is ugly, as you would expect. And Napoleon's doesn't seem to know where to stop; how much like the man!

I think my father was right when he said handwriting was often the key to a man's character, and that large well-formed letters went with an uncluttered mind. Florence Nightingale had a lovely handwriting, the hand of a caring person. And there were many like her, amongst our forebears.

3
WORDS AND PICTURES

When I was a small boy, no Christmas was really complete unless my Christmas stocking contained several recent issues of my favourite comic-paper. If today my friends complain that I am too voracious a reader of books, they have only these comics to blame; for they were the origin, if not of my tastes in reading, then certainly of the reading habit itself.

I like to think that my conversion to comics began at the age of five, with a comic strip on the children's page of *The*

Statesman. In the late 1930s, Benji, whose head later appeared only on the Benji League badge, had a strip to himself; I don't remember his adventures very clearly, but every day (or was it once a week?) I would cut out the Benji strip and paste it into a scrapbook. Two years later this scrapbook, bursting with the adventures of Benji, accompanied me to boarding school, where, of course, it passed through several hands before finally passing into limbo.

Of course comics did not form the only reading matter that found its way into my Christmas stocking. Before I was eight, I had read *Peter Pan*, *Alice*, and most of *Mr. Midshipman Easy*; but I had also consumed thousands of comic-papers which were, after all, slim affairs and mostly pictorial, 'certain little penny books radiant with gold and rich with bad pictures', as Leigh Hunt described the children's papers of his own time.

But though they were mostly pictorial, comics in those days did have a fair amount of reading matter, too. *The Hostspur*, *Wizard*, *Magnet* (a victim of the Second World War) and *Champion* contained stories woven round certain popular characters. In *Champion*, which I read regularly right through my prep school years, there was Rockfist Rogan, Royal Air Force (R.A.F.), a pugilist who managed to combine boxing with bombing, and Fireworks Flynn, a footballer who always scored the winning-goal in the last two minutes of play.

Billy Bunter has, of course, become one of the immortals,—almost a subject for literary and social historians.

Quite recently, *The Times Literary Supplement* devoted its first two pages to an analysis of the Bunter stories. Eminent lawyers and doctors still look back nostalgically to the arrival of the weekly *Magnet*; they are now the principal customers for the special souvenir edition of the first issue of the *Magnet*, recently reprinted in facsimile. Bunter, 'forever young', has become a folk hero. He is seen on stage, screen and television, and is even quoted in the House of Commons.

From this, I take courage. My only regret is that I did not preserve my own early comics—not because of any bibliophilic value which they might possess today, but because of my sentimental regard for early influences in art and literature.

The first venture in children's publishing, in 1774 was a comic of sorts. In that year, John Newberry brought out:

According to Act of Parliament (neatly bound and gilt): A Little Pretty Pocket-Book, intended for the Instruction and Amusement of Little Master Tommy and Pretty Miss Polly, with an agreeable Letter to read from Jack the Giant-Killer...

The book contained pictures, rhymes and games. Newberry's characters and imaginary authors included Woglog the Giant, Tommy Trip, Giles Gingerbread, Nurse Truelove, Peregrine Puzzlebrains, Primrose Prettyface, and many others with names similar to those found in the comic-papers of our own century.

Newberry was also the originator of the 'Amazing Free Offer', so much a part of American comics. At the beginning of 1755, he had this to offer:

Nurse Truelove's New Year Gift, or the Book of Books for children, adorned with Cuts and designed as a Present for every little boy who would become a great Man and ride upon a fine Horse; and to every little Girl who would become a great Woman and ride in a Lord Mayor's gilt Coach. Printed for the Author, who has ordered these books to be given gratis to all little Boys in St. Paul's churchyard, they paying for the Binding, which is only Two pence each Book.

Many of today's comics are crude and, like many television serials violent in their appeal. But I did not know American comics until I was twelve, and by then I had become quite discriminating. Superman, Bulletman, Batman, and Green Lantern, and other super heroes all left me cold. I had, by then, passed into the world of real books but the weakness for the comic strip remains. I no longer receive comics in my Christmas stocking; but I do place a few in the stockings of Gautam and Siddharth. And, needless to say, I read them right through beforehand.

Thirteen

To Light a Fire

To light a fire
We must kneel.
To change a tyre,
We must descend;
To pluck a flower,
We bend;
To lift a child,
We bend again;
To touch an elder's feet
We do the same.
For prayer, or play, or just plain mending,
There's something to be said for bending!

Fourteen

A Song of Many Rivers

When I look down from the heights of Landour to broad valley of the Doon far below, I can see the little Suswa river, silver in the setting sun, meandering through fields and forests on its way to its confluence with the Ganga.

The Suswa is a river I knew well as a boy, but it has been many years since I took a dip in its quiet pools or rested in the shade of the tall spreading trees growing on its banks. Now I see it from my windows, far away, dreamlike in the mist, and I keep promising myself that I will visit it again, to touch its waters, cool and clear, and feel its rounded pebbles beneath my feet.

It's a little river, flowing down from the ancient Siwaliks and running the length of the valley until, with its sister river the Song, it slips into the Ganga just above the holy city of Hardwar. I could wade across (except during the monsoon when it was in spate) and the water seldom rose above the waist except in sheltered pools, where there were shoals of small fish.

There is a little known and charming legend about the Suswa and its origins, which I have always treasured. It tells us that the Hindu sage, Kasyapa, once gave a great feast to which all the gods were invited. Now Indra, the God of Rain, while on his way to the entertainment, happened to meet 60,000 *'balkhils'* (pygmies) of the Brahmin caste, who were trying in vain to cross a cow's footprint filled with water—to them, a vast lake!

The god could not restrain his amusement. Peals of thunderous laughter echoed across the hills. The indignant Brahmins, determined to have their revenge, at once set to work creating a second Indra, who should supplant the reigning god. This could only be done by means of penance, fasting and self-denial, in which they persevered until the sweat flowing from their tiny bodies created the 'Suswa' or 'flowing waters' of the little river.

Indra, alarmed at the effect of these religious exercises, sought the help of Brahma, the creator, who taking on the role of a referee, interceded with the priests. Indra was able to keep his position as the rain god.

I saw no pygmies or fairies near the Suswa, but I did see many spotted deer, cheetal, coming down to the water's edge to drink. They are still plentiful in that area.

2
THE NAUTCH GIRL'S CURSE

At the other end of the Doon, far to the west, the Yamuna comes down from the mountains and forms the boundary between the states of Himachal and Uttaranchal. Today, there's a bridge across the river, but many years ago, when I first went across, it was by means of a small cable car, and a very rickety one at that.

During the monsoon, when the river was in spate, the only way across the swollen river was by means of this swaying trolley, which was suspended by a steel rope to two shaky wooden platforms on either bank. There followed a tedious bus journey, during which some sixty odd miles were covered in six hours. And then you were at Nahan, a small town a little over 3,000 feet above sea level, set amidst hill slopes thick with sal and shisham trees. This charming old town links the subtropical Siwaliks to the first foothills of the Himalaya, a unique situation.

The road from Dagshai and Shimla runs into Nahan from the north. No matter in which direction you look, the view is a fine one. To the south stretches the grand panorama of the plains of Saharanpur and Ambala, fronted by two low ranges of thickly forested hills. In the valley below, the pretty Markanda river winds its way out of the Kadir valley.

Nahan's main street is curved and narrow, but well-made and paved with good stone. To the left of the town is the former Raja's palace. Nahan was once the capital of the state of Sirmur, now part of Himachal Pradesh. The original palace was built some three or four hundred years ago, but has been added to from time to time, and is now a large collection of buildings mostly in the Venetian style.

I suppose Nahan qualifies as a hill station, although it can be quite hot in summer. But unlike most hill stations, which are less than two hundred years old, Nahan is steeped in legend and history.

The old capital of Sirmur was destroyed by an earthquake some seven to eight hundred years ago. It was situated some twenty-four miles from present-day Nahan, on the west bank of the Giri, where the river expands into a lake. The ancient capital was totally destroyed, with all its inhabitants, and apparently no record was left of its then ruling family. Little remained of the ancient city, just a ruined temple and a few broken stone figures.

As to the cause of the tragedy, the traditional story is that a nautch girl happened to visit Sirmur, and performed some wonderful feats. The Raja challenged the girl to walk safely over the Giri on a rope, offering her half his kingdom if she was successful.

The girl accepted the challenge. A rope was stretched across the river. But before starting out, the girl promised that if she fell victim to any treachery on the part of the Raja, a curse would fall upon the city and it would be destroyed by a terrible catastrophe.

While she was on her way to successfully carrying out the

feat, some of the Raja's people cut the rope. She fell into the river and was drowned. As predicted, total destruction came to the town.

The founder of the next line of the Sirmur Raja came from the Jaisalmer family in Rajasthan. He was on a pilgrimage to Hardwar with his wife when he heard of the catastrophe that had immolated every member of the state's ancient dynasty. He went at once with his wife into the territory, and established a Jaisalmer Raj. The descent from the first Rajput ruler of Jaisalmer stock, some seven hundred years ago, followed from father to son in an unbroken line. And after much intitial moving about, Nahan was fixed upon as the capital.

The territory was captured by the Gurkhas in 1803, but twelve years later, they were expelled by the British after some severe fighting, to which a small English cemetery bears witness. The territory was restored to the Raja, with the exception of the Jaunsar Bawar region.

Six or seven miles north of Nahan lies the mountain of Jaitak, where the Gurkhas made their last desperate stand. The place is worth a visit, not only for seeing the remains of the Gurkha fort, but also for the magnificent view the mountain commands.

From the northernmost of the mountain's twin peaks, the whole south face of the Himalayas may be seen. From west to north you see the rugged prominences of the Jaunsar Bawar, flanked by the Mussoorie range of hills. It is wild mountain scenery, with a few patches of cultivation and little villages nestling on the sides of the hills. Garhwal and Dehradun are to the east, and as you go downhill you can see the broad sweep of the Yamuna as it cuts its way through the western Siwaliks.

3
GENTLY FLOWS THE GANGA

The Bhagirathi is a beautiful river, gentle and caressing (as compared to the turbulent Alaknanda), and pilgrims and others have responded to it with love and respect. The God Shiva released the waters of Goddess Ganga from his locks, and she sped towards the plains in the tracks of Prince Bhagirath's chariot.

> He held the river on his head
> And kept her wandering, where
> Dense as Himalaya's woods were spread
> The tangles of his hair.

Revered by Hindus and loved by all, Goddess Ganga weaves her spell over all who come to her.

Some assert that the true Ganga (in its upper reaches) is the Alaknanda. Geographically, this may be so. But tradition carries greater weight in the abode of the Gods and traditionally the Bhagirathi is the Ganga. Of course, the two rivers meet at Devprayag, in the foothills, and this marriage of the waters settles the issue.

Here, at the source of the river, we come to the realization that we are at the very centre and heart of things. One has an almost primaeval sense of belonging to these mountains arid to this valley in particular. For me, and for many who have been here, the Bhagirathi is the most beautiful of the four main river valleys of Garhwal.

The Bhagirathi seems to have everything—a gentle disposition, deep glens and forests, the ultravision of an open valley graced with tiers of cultivation leading up by degrees to the peaks and glaciers at its head.

At Tehri, the big dam slows down Prince Bhagirath's chariot. But upstream, from Bhatwari to Harsil, there are extensive pine forests. They fill the ravines and plateaus, before giving way to yew and cypress, oak and chestnut. Above 9,000 feet the deodar (devdar, tree of the gods) is the principal tree. It grows to a little distance above Gangotri, and then gives way to the birch, which is found in patches to within half a mile of the glacier.

It was the valuable timber of the deodar that attracted the adventurer Frederick 'Pahari' Wilson to the valley in the 1850s. He leased the forests from the Raja of Tehri, and within a few years he had made a fortune. From his home and depot at Harsil, he would float the logs downstream to Tehri, where diey would be sawn up and despatched to buyers in the cities.

Bridge-building was another of Wilson's ventures. The most famous of these was a 350-feet suspension bridge at Bhaironghat, over 1,200 feet above the young Bhagirathi where it thunders through a deep defile. This rippling contraption was at first a source of terror to travellers, and only a few ventured across it. To reassure people, Wilson would mount his horse and gallop to and fro across the bridge. It has since collapsed, but local people will tell you that the ghostly hoof beats of Wilson's horse can still be heard on full moon nights. The supports of the old bridge were massive deodar trunks, and they can still be seen to one side of the new road bridge built by engineers of the Northern Railway.

Wilson married a local girl, Gulabi, the daughter of a drummer from Mukbha, a village a few miles above Harsil. He acquired properties in Dehradun and Mussoorie, and his wife lived there in some style, giving him three sons. Two died young. The third, Charlie Wilson, went through most of his father's fortune. His grave lies next to my grandfather's grave in the old Dehradun cemetery. Gulabi is buried in Mussoorie, next to her husband. I wrote this haiku for her:

> Her beauty brought her fame,
> But only the wild rose growing beside her grave
> Is there to hear her whispered name—
> Gulabi.

I remember old Mrs Wilson, Charlie's widow, when I was a boy in Dehra. She lived next door in what was the last of the Wilson properties. Her nephew, Geoffrey Davis, went to school with me in Shimla, and later joined the Indian Air Force. But luck never went the way of Wilson's descendants, and Geoffrey died when his plane crashed.

In the old days, before motorable roads opened up the border states, only the staunchest of pilgrims visited the shrines at Gangotri and elsewhere. The footpaths were rocky and dangerous, ascending and descending the faces of deep precipices and ravines, at times leading along banks of loose earth where landslides had swept the original path away. There are no big towns above Uttarkashi, and this absence of large centres of population could be the main reason why the forests are better preserved here than at lower altitudes.

Uttarkashi is a sizeable town but situated between two steep hills, it gives one a cramped, shut-in feeling. Fifteen years ago it was devastated by a major earthquake, and in recent months it has suffered from repeated landslides. Somehow its situation seems far from ideal.

Gangotri, far more secure, is situated at just over 10,300 feet. On the right bank of the river is the principal temple, a small neat shrine without much ornamentation. It was built by Amar Singh Thapa, a Nepali general, in the early 1800s. It was renovated by the Maharaja of Jaipur in 1920. The rock on which it stands is called Bhagirath Shila and is said to be the place where Prince Bhagirath did penance in order that Ganga be brought down from her abode of eternal snow.

Here the rocks are carved and polished by ice and water, so smooth that in places they look like rolls of silk. The fast flowing waters of this mountain torrent look very different from the huge, sluggish river that joins the Yamuna at Allahabad.

The Ganga emerges from beneath a great glacier, thickly studded with enormous loose rocks and earth. The glacier is about a mile in width and extends upwards for many miles. The chasm in the glacier, from which the stream rushes forth into the light of day, is named Gaumukh, the cow's mouth, and is held in deepest reverence by Hindus. This region of eternal frost was the scene of many of their most sacred mysteries.

At Gangotri, the Ganga is no puny stream, but is already a river thirty or forty yards wide. At Gauri Kund, below the temple, it falls over a rock of considerable height, and continues tumbling over a succession of small cascades until it enters the Bhaironghat gorge.

A night spent beside the river is an eerie experience. After some time it begins to sound, not like one fall but a hundred, and this sound is ever-present both in one's dreams and waking hours.

Rising early to greet the dawn proved rather pointless, as the surrounding peaks did not let the sun in till after 9 a.m. Everyone rushed about to keep warm, exclaiming delightedly at what they described as *gulabi thand*, literally 'rosy cold'. Guaranteed to turn the cheeks a rosy pink! A charming expression, but I prefer a rosy sunburn and remained beneath a heavy quilt until the sun came up over the mountain to throw its golden shafts across the river.

This is mid-October, and after Diwali the shrine and the small township will close for the winter, the pandits retreating to the relative warmth of Mukbha. Soon snow will cover everything, and even the hardy purple plumaged whistling thrushes (known here as *hastura*), who are lovers of deep shade, will move further down the valley. And further down, below the forest line, the hardy Garhwali farmers will go about harvesting their terraced fields which form patterns of yellow, green and gold above the deep green of the river.

Yes, the Bhagirathi is a green river. Although deep and swift, it has a certain serenity. At no place does it look hurried or confused—unlike the turbulent Alaknanda, fretting and fuming as it crashes down its boulder-strewn bed. The Bhagirathi is free-flowing, at peace with itself and its devotees. At all times and places, it seems to find a true and harmonious balance.

✧

4
FALLING FOR MANDAKINI

A great river at its confluence with another great river is, for me, a special moment in time. And so it was with the Mandakini at Rudraprayag, where its waters joined the waters of the Alaknanda, the one having come from the glacial snows above Kedarnath, the other from the Himalayan heights beyond Badrinath. Both sacred rivers, destined to become the holy Ganga further downstream.

I fell in love with the Mandakini at first sight. Or was it the valley that I fell in love with? I am not sure, and it doesn't really matter. The valley is the river.

While the Alaknanda valley, especially in its higher reaches, is a deep and narrow gorge where precipitous outcrops of rock hang threateningly over the traveller, the Mandakini valley is broader, gentler, the terraced fields wider, the banks of the river a green sward in many places. Somehow, one does not feel that one is at the mercy of the Mandakini whereas one is always at the mercy of the Alaknanda with its sudden floods.

Rudraprayag is hot. It is probably a pleasant spot in winter, but at the end of June, it is decidedly hot. Perhaps its chief claim to fame is that it gave its name to the dreaded man-eating leopard of Rudraprayag who, in the course of seven years (1918–25), accounted for more than 300 victims. It was finally shot by Jim Corbett, who recounted the saga of his long hunt for the killer in his fine book, *The Man-eating Leopard of Rudraprayag*.

The place at which the leopard was shot was the (village of Gulabrai, two miles south of Rudraprayag. Under a large mango tree stands a memorial raised to Jim Corbett by officers and men of the Border Roads Organisation. It is a touching gesture to one who loved Garhwal and India. Unfortunately, several buffaloes are tethered close by, and one has to wade through slush and buffalo dung to get to the memorial stone. A board tacked on to the mango tree attracts the attention of motorists who might pass without noticing the memorial, which is off to one side.

The killer leopard was noted for its direct method of attack on humans; and, in spite of being poisoned, trapped in a cave, and shot at innumerable times, it did not lose its contempt for man. Two English sportsmen covering both ends to the old suspension bridge over the Alaknanda fired several times at the man-eater but to little effect.

It was not long before the leopard acquired a reputation among the hill folk for being an evil spirit. A sadhu was suspected of turning into the leopard by night, and was only saved from being lynched by the ingenuity of Philip Mason, then deputy commissioner of Garhwal. Mason kept the sadhu in custody until the leopard made his next attack, thus proving the man innocent. Years later, when Mason turned novelist and (using the pen name Philip Woodruffe) wrote *The Wild Sweet Witch*, he had one of the characters, a beautiful young woman who apparently turns into a man-eating leopard by night.

Corbett's host at Gulabrai was one of the few who survived an encounter with the leopard. It left him with a hole in his throat. Apart from being a superb storyteller, Corbett displayed great compassion for people from all walks of life and is still a legend in Garhwal and Kumaon amongst people who have never read his books.

In June, one does not linger long in the steamy heat of Rudraprayag. But as one travels up the river, making a gradual ascent of the Mandakini valley, there is a cool breeze coming down from the snows, and the smell of rain is in the air.

The thriving little township of Agastmuni spreads itself along the wide river banks. Further upstream, near a little place called Chandrapuri, we cannot resist breaking our journey to sprawl on the tender green grass that slopes gently down to the swift flowing river. A small rest-house is in the making. Around it, banana fronds sway and poplar leaves dance in the breeze.

This is no sluggish river of the plains, but a fast-moving current, tumbling over rocks, turning and twisting in its efforts to discover the easiest way for its frothy snow-fed waters to escape the mountains. Escape is the word! For the constant plaint of many a Garhwali is that, while his hills abound in rivers, the water runs down and away, and little if any reaches the fields and villages above it. Cultivation must depend on the rain and not on the river.

The road climbs gradually, still keeping to the river. Just outside Guptakashi, my attention is drawn to a clump of huge trees sheltering a small but ancient temple. We stop here and enter the shade of the trees.

The temple is deserted. It is a temple dedicated to Shiva, and in the courtyard are several river-rounded stone lingams on which leaves and blossoms have fallen. No one seems to come here, which is strange, since it is on the pilgrim route. Two boys from a neighbouring field leave their yoked bullocks to come and talk to me, but they cannot tell me much about the temple except to confirm that it is seldom visited. 'The buses do not stop here.' That seems explanation enough. For where the buses go, the pilgrims go; and where the pilgrims go' other pilgrims will follow. Thus far and no further.

The trees seem to be magnolias. But I have never seen magnolia trees grow to such huge proportions. Perhaps they are something else. Never mind; let them remain a mystery.

Guptakashi in the evening is all a bustle. A coachload of pilgrims (headed for Kedarnath) has just arrived, and the tea shops near the bus stand are doing brisk business. Then the 'local' bus from Ukhimath, across the river arrives, and many of the passengers head for a tea shop famed for its samosas. The local bus is called the Bhook-Hartal, the 'Hunger strike' bus.

'How did it get that name?' I asked one of the samosa-eaters.

'Well, it's an interesting story. For a long time we had been asking the authorities to provide a bus service for the local people and for the villagers who live off the roads. All the buses came from Srinagar or Rishikesh, and were taken up by pilgrims. The locals couldn't find room in them. But our pleas went unheard until the whole town, or most of it, decided to go on hunger strike.'

'They nearly put me out of business too,' said the tea-shop owner cheerfully. 'Nobody ate any samosas for two days!'

There is no cinema or public place of entertainment at Guptakashi, and the town goes to sleep early. And wakes up early.

At six, the hillside, green from recent rain, sparkles in the morning sunshine. Snowcapped Chaukhamba (7,140 meters) is dazzling. The air is clear; no smoke or dust up here. The climate, I am told, is mild all the year round judging by the scent and shape of the flowers, and the boys call them Champs, Hindi for champa blossom. Ukhimath, on the other side of the river, lies in the shadow. It gets the sun at nine. In winter, it must wait till afternoon.

Guptakashi has not yet been rendered ugly by the barrack type architecture that has come up in some growing hill towns. The old double storeyed houses are built of stone, with grey slate roofs. They blend well with the hillside. Cobbled paths meander through the old bazaar.

One of these takes up to the famed Guptakashi temple, tucked away above the old part of the town. Here, as in Benaras, Shiva is worshipped as Vishwanath, and two underground streams representing the sacred Jamuna and Bhagirathi rivers feed the pool sacred to the God. This temple gives the town its name, Gupta-Kashi, the 'Invisible Benaras', just as Uttarkashi on the Bhagirathi is 'Upper Benaras.'

Guptakashi and its environs have so many lingams that the saying *'Jitne kankar utne shankar'*—'As many stones, so many Shivas'—has become a proverb to describe its holiness.

From Guptakashi, pilgrims proceed north to Kedarnath, and the last stage of their journey—about a day's march—must be covered on foot or horseback. The temple of Kedarnath, situated at a height of 11.753 feet, is encircled by snowcapped peaks, and Atkinson has conjectured that 'the symbol of the linga may have arisen from the pointed peaks around his (God Shiva's) original home'.

The temple is dedicated to Sadashiva, the subterranean form of the God, who, 'fleeing from the Pandavas took refuge here in the form of a he-buffalo and finding himself hard-pressed, dived into the ground leaving the hinder parts on the surface, which continue to be the subject of adoration.' (Atkinson).

The other portions of the God are worshipped as follows—the arms at Tungnath, at a height of 13,000 feet, the face at Rudranath (12,000 feet), the belly at Madrnaheshwar, 18 miles northeast of Guptakashi; and the hair and head at Kalpeshwar, near Joshimath. These five sacred shrines form the *Panch Kedars* (five *Kedars*).

We leave the Mandakini to visit Tungnath on the Chandrashila range. But I will return to this river. It has captured my mind and heart.

Fifteen

My Far Pavilions

Bright red
The poinsettia flames,
As autumn and the old year wanes.

WHEN I HAVE TIME ON MY HANDS, I WRITE haikus, like the one above. This one brings back memories and images of my maternal grandmother's home in Dehradun, in the early 1940s. I say grandmother's home because, although grandfather built the house, he had passed on while I was still a child and I have no memories of him that I can conjure up. But he was someone about whom everyone spoke, and I learnt that he had personally supervised the building of the house, partially designing it on the lines of a typical Indian Railways bungalow—neat, compact, and without any frills. None of those Doric pillars, Gothic arches, and mediaeval turrets that characterized some of the Raj house for an earlier period. But instead of the customary red bricks, he used the smooth rounded stones from a local riverbed, and this gave the bungalow a distinctive look.

In all the sixty-five years that I have lived in India, my grandparents' abode was the only house that gave me a feeling of some permanence, as neither my parents nor I were ever to own property. But India was my home, and it was big enough.

Grandfather looked after the mango and lichi orchard at the back of the house, grandmother looked after the flower garden in front. English flowers predominated—philox, larkspur, petunias, sweet peas, snapdragons, nasturtiums; but there was also a jasmine bush, poinsettias, and of course, lots of colourful bougainvillaea climbing the walls. And there were roses brought over from nearby Saharanpur. Saharanpur had become a busy railway junction and an industrial town, but its roses were still famous. It was the home of the botanical survey in northern India, and in the previous century many famous botanists and explorers had ventured into the Himalayas using Saharanpur as their base.

Grandfather had retired from the Railways and settled in Dehra around 1905. At this period, the small foothills town was becoming quite popular as a retreat for retiring Anglo-Indian and domiciled Europeans. The bungalows had large compounds and gardens, and Dehra was to remain a garden town until a few years after Independence. The Forest Research Institute, the Survey of India, the Indian Military Academy, and a number of good schools, made the town a special sort of place. By the mid-fifties, the pressures of population meant a greater demand for housing, and gradually the large compounds gave way to housing estates, and the gardens and orchards began to disappear. Most of the estates were now owned by the prospering Indian middle classes. Some of them strove to maintain the town's character and unique charm—flower shows, dog shows, school fetes, club life, dances, garden parties—but gradually these diminished; and today, as the capital of the new state of Uttaranchal, Dehra is as busy, congested and glamorous as any northern town or New Delhi suburb.

My father was always on the move. As a young man, he had been a schoolteacher at Lovedale, in the Nilgiris, then an assistant manager on a tea estate in Travancore-Cochin (now Kerala). He had also worked in the Ichhapore Rifle Factory bordering Calcutta. At the time I was born, he was employed in the Kathiawar states, setting up little schools for the state children in Jamnagar, Pithadia and Jetpur. I grew up in a variety of dwellings, ranging from leaky old dak bungalows to spacious palace guesthouses. Then, during the Second World War, when he enlisted and was posted in Delhi, we moved from tent to Air Force hutment, to a flat in Scindia House, to rented rooms on Hailey Road, Atul Grove, and elsewhere! When he was posted to Karachi, and then Calcutta, I was sent to boarding school in Shimla.

Father had, in fact, grown up in Calcutta, and his mother still lived at 14, Park Lane. She outlived all her children and continued to live at Park Lane until she was almost ninety. Last year, when I visited Calcutta, I found the Park Lane house. But it was boarded up. Nobody seemed to live there any more.

Garbage was piled up near the entrance. A billboard hid most of the house from the road.

Possibly, my boarding school, Bishop Cotton's in Shimla, provided me with a certain feeling of permanence, especially after I lost my father in 1944. Known as the 'Eton of the East', and run on English public school lines, Bishop Cotton's did not cater to individual privacy. Everyone knew what you kept in your locker. But when I became a senior, I was fortunate enough to be put in charge of the school library. I could use it in my free time, and it became my retreat, where I could read or write or just be on my own. No one bothered me there, for even in those pre-TV and pre-computer days there was no great demand for books! Reading was a minority pastime then, as it is now.

After school, when I was trying to write and sell my early short stories, I found myself ensconced in a tiny *barsati*, a room on the roof of an old lodging house in Dehradun. Alas! Granny's house had been sold by her eldest daugher, who had gone 'home' to England; my stepfather's home was full of half-brothers, stepbrothers and sundry relatives. The *barsati* gave me privacy.

A bed, a table and a chair were all that the room contained. It was all I needed. Even today, almost fifty years later, my room has the same basic furnishings, except that the table is larger, the bed is slightly more comfortable, and there is a rug on the floor, designed to trip me up whenever I sally forth from the room.

Then, as now, the view from the room, or from its windows, has always been an important factor in my life. I don't think I could stay anywhere for long unless I had a window from which to gaze out upon the world.

Dehradun isn't very far from where I live today, and I have passed granny's old bungalow quite often. It is really half a house now, a wall having been built through the centre of the compound. Like the country itself, it found itself partitioned, and there are two owners; one has the lichi trees and the other the mangoes. Good luck to both!

I do not venture in at the gate, I shall keep my memories intact. The only reminders of the past are a couple of potted geraniums on the verandah steps. And I shall sign off with another little haiku:

Red geranium

Gleaming against the rain-bright floor...
Memory, hold the door!

Sixteen

Return to Dehra

This is old Dehra
Of mangoes and lemons
Where I grew up
Beside the jacaranda
Planted by my father
On the sunny side
Of the long veranda.
This is the house
Since sold
To Major-General Mehra.
The town has grown,
None knows me now
Who knew
My mother's laughter.
Most men come home as strangers.
And yet,
The trees my father planted here—
These spreading trees—
Are still at home in Dehra.

Seventeen

Joyfully I Write

I AM A FORTUNATE PERSON. FOR OVER FIFTY years I have been able to make a living by doing what I enjoy most—writing.

Sometimes I wonder if I have written too much. One gets into the habit of serving up the same ideas over and over again; with a different sauce perhaps, but still the same ideas, themes, memories, characters. Writers are often chided for repeating themselves. Artists and musicians are given more latitude. No one criticized Turner for painting so many sunsets at sea, or Gauguin for giving us all those lovely Tahitian women; or Husain, for treating us to so many horses, or Jamini Roy for giving us so many identical stylized figures.

In the world of music, one Puccini opera is very like another, a Chopin nocturne will return to familiar themes, and in the realm of lighter, modern music the same melodies recur with only slight variations. But authors are often taken to task for repeating themselves. They cannot help this, for in their writing they are expressing their personalities. Hemingway's world is very different from Jane Austen's. They are both unique worlds, but they do not change or mutate in the minds of their author-creators. Jane Austen spent all her life in one small place, and portrayed the people she knew. Hemingway roamed the world, but his characters remained much the same, usually extensions of himself.

In the course of a long writing career, it is inevitable that a writer will occasionally repeat himself, or return to themes that have remained with him even as new ideas and formulations enter his mind. The important thing is to keep writing, observing, listening, and paying attention to the beauty of words and their arrangement. And like artists and musicians, the more we work on our art, the better it will be.

Writing, for me, is the simplest and greatest pleasure in the world. Putting a mood or an idea into words is an occupation I truly love. I plan my day so that there is time in it for writing a poem, or a paragraph, or an essay, or part of a story or longer work; not just because writing is my profession, but from a feeling of delight.

The world around me—be it the mountains or the busy street below my window—is teeming with subjects, sights, thoughts, that I wish to put into words in order to catch the fleeting moment, the passing image, the laughter, the joy, and sometimes the sorrow. Life would be intolerable if I did not have this freedom to write every day. Not that everything I put down is worth preserving. A great many pages of manuscripts have found their way into my wastepaper basket or into the stove that warms the family room on cold winter evenings. I do not always please myself. I cannot always please others because, unlike the hard professionals, the Forsyths and the Sheldons, I am not writing to please everyone, I am really writing to please myself!

My theory of writing is that the conception should be as clear as possible, and that words should flow like a stream of clear water, preferably a mountain-stream! You will, of cottrse, encounter boulders, but you will learn to go over them or around them, so that your flow is unimpeded. If your stream gets too sluggish or muddy, it is better to put aside that particular piece of writing. Go to the source, go to the spring, where the water is purest, your thoughts as clear as the mountain air.

I do not write for more than an hour or two in the course of the day. Too long at the desk, and words lose their freshness.

Together with clarity and a good vocabulary, there must come a certain elevation of mood. Sterne must have been bubbling over with high spirits when he wrote *Shandy*. The sombre intensity of *Wuthering Heights* reflects Emily Brontë's passion for life, fully knowing that it was to be brief. Tagore's melancholy comes through in his poetry. Dickens is always passionate; there are no half measures in his work. Conrad's prose takes on the moods of the sea he knew and loved.

A real physical emotion accompanies the process of writing, and great writers are those who can channel this emotion into the creation of their best work.

'Are you a serious writer?' a schoolboy once asked.

'Well, I try to be serious,' I said, 'but cheerfulness keeps breaking in!'

Can a cheerful writer be taken seriously? I don't know. But I was certainly serious about making writing the main occupation of my life.

In order to do this, one has to give up many things—a job, security, comfort, domesticity—or rather, the pursuit of these things. Had I married when I was twenty-five, I would not have been able to throw up a good job as easily as I did at the time; I might now be living on a pension! God forbid. I am grateful for continued independence and the necessity to keep writing for my living, and for those who share their lives with me and whose joys and sorrows are mine too. An artist must not lose his hold on life. We do that when we settle for the safety of a comfortable old age.

Normally writers do not talk much, because they are saving their conversation for the readers of their books—those invisible listeners with whom we wish to strike a sympathetic chord. Of course, we talk freely with our friends, but we are reserved with people we do not know very well. If I talk too freely about a story I am going to write, chances are it will never be written. I have talked it to death.

Being alone is vital for any creative writer. I do not mean that you must live the life of a recluse. People who do not know me are frequently under the impression that I live in lonely splendour on a mountaintop, whereas in reality, I share a small flat with a family of twelve—and I'm the twelfth man, occasionally bringing out refreshments for the players!

I love my extended family, every single individual in it, but as a writer I must sometimes get a little time to be alone with my own thoughts, reflect a little, talk to myself, laugh about all the blunders I have committed in the past, and ponder over the future. This is contemplation, not meditation. I am not very good at meditation, as it involves remaining in a passive state for some time. I would rather be out walking, observing the natural world, or sitting under a tree contemplating my novel or navel! I suppose the latter is a form of meditation.

When I casually told a journalist that I planned to write a book consisting of my meditations, he reported that I was writing a book on meditation per se, which gave it a different connotation. I shall go along with the simple dictionary meaning of the verb meditate—to plan mentally, to exercise the mind in contemplation.

So I was doing it all along!

I am not, by nature, a gregarious person. Although I love people, and have often made friends with complete strangers, I am also a lover of solitude. Naturally, one thinks better when one is alone. But I prefer walking alone to walking with others. That ladybird on the wild rose would escape my attention if I was engaged in a lively conversation with a companion. Not that the ladybird is going to change my life. But by acknowledging its presence, stopping to admire its beauty, I have paid obeisance to the natural scheme of things of which I am only a small part.

It is upon a person's power of holding fast to such un dimmed beauty that his or her inner hopefulness depends. As we journey through the world, we must inevitably encounter meanness and selfishness. As we fight for our survival, the higher visions and ideals often fade. It is then that we need ladybirds! Contemplating that tiny creature, or the flower on which it rests, gives one the hope—better, the certainty— that there is more to life than interest rates, dividends, market forces, and infinite technology.

As a writer, I have known hope and despair, success and failure; some recognition but also long periods of neglect and critical dismissal. But I have had no regrets. I have enjoyed the writer's life to the full, and one reason for this is that living in India has given me certain freedoms which I would not have enjoyed elsewhere. Friendship when needed. Solitude when desired. Even, at times, love and passion. It has tolerated me for what I am—a bit of a dropout, unconventional, idiosyncratic. I have been left alone to do my own thing. In India, people do not censure you unless you start making a nuisance of yourself. Society has its norms and its orthodoxies, and provided you do not flaunt all the rules, society will allow you to go your own way. I am free to become a naked ascetic and roam the streets with a begging bowl; I am also free to live in a palatial farmhouse if I have the wherewithal. For twenty-five years, I have lived in this small, sunny second-floor room looking out on the mountains, and no one has bothered me, unless you count the neighbour's dog who prevents the postman and courier boys from coming up the steps.

I may write for myself, but as I also write to get published, it must follow that I write for others too. Only a handful of readers might enjoy my writing, but they are my soul mates, my alter egos, and they keep me going through those lean times and discouraging moments.

Even though I depend upon my writing for a livelihood, it is still, for me, the most delightful thing in the world.

I did not set out to make a fortune from writing; I knew I was not that kind of writer. But it was the thing I did best, and I persevered with the exercise of my gift, cultivating the more discriminating editors, publishers and readers, never really expecting huge rewards but accepting whatever came my way. Happiness is a matter of temperament rather than circumstance, and I have always considered myself fortunate in having escaped the tedium of a nine-to-five job or some other form of drudgery.

Of course, there comes a time when almost every author asks himself what his effort and output really amounts to? We expect our work to influence people, to affect a great many readers, when in fact, its impact is infinitesimal. Those who work on a large scale must feel discouraged by the world's indifference. That is why I am happy to give a little innocent pleasure to a handful of readers. This is a reward worth having.

As a writer, I have difficulty in doing justice to momentous events, the wars of nations, the politics of power; I am more at ease with the dew of the morning, the sensuous delights of the day, the silent blessings of the night, the joys and sorrows of children, the strivings of ordinary folk, and of course, the ridiculous situations in which we sometimes find ourselves.

We cannot prevent sorrow and pain and tragedy. And yet, when we look around us, we find that the majority of people are actually enjoying life! There are so many lovely things to see, there is so much to do, so much fun to be had, and so many charming and interesting people to meet... How can my pen ever run dry?

Eighteen

His Last Words

Seeing Ananda weeping, Gautama said,
'Do not weep, Ananda. This body of ours
Contains within itself the powers
Which renew its strength for a time
But also that which leads to its destruction.
Is there anything put together
Which shall not dissolve?'
And turning to his disciples, he said,
'When I am no longer with you,
I will still be in your midst.
You have my laws, my words, my very essence.
Beloved disciples,
If you love my memory, love one another.
I called you to tell you this.'

These were the last words of the Buddha
As he stretched himself out
And slept the final sleep
Under the great Sal tree
At Kusinagara.

Nineteen

Thoughts on Approaching Seventy

'**W**HAT DOES IT FEEL LIKE TO BE SEVENTY?' asked a young friend, just the other day.

'No different to what it felt like to be seventeen,' I replied. And, as an afterthought, added, 'Except that I can't climb trees any more.'

Not that I was ever much good at climbing trees, or riding bicycles or ponies, doing the high jump, climbing ropes, or doing the swallow dive. My best effort at the swimming pool was a belly flop which emptied half the pool.

No, I was never very supple or acrobatic. But I could walk long distances, and still can on a fine day, and it was probably this ability to plod on, over hill and dale, that has enabled me to be here today, at the fast approaching age of three score and ten.

I have never been a fitness freak, and my figure would not

get me into the chorus line of a Bollywood musical. I won't bore the reader with details of my eating habits except to say that I eat and drink what I like, and if I am still functioning reasonably well at seventy, it has more to do with the good fresh air of the hills than to any regimen of diet and exercie. 'Honour your food,' said Manu the lawgiver, 'receive it thankfully, do not hold it in contempt.'

Living forever is not one of my ambitions. Life is wonderful and one would like to have as much of it as possible. But there comes a time when mind and body must succumb to the many years of strife and struggle. When I look in the mirror (something that is to be avoided as much as possible), I see definite signs of wear and tear. This is only natural. Flowers fade, wither away. So must humans. But if the seed is good, other flowers, other people will take our place.

Beware of second-hand mirrors. I bought one once, from Vinod's antique shop. He told me it had belonged to a wicked old Begum or Maharani who had done away with several of her paramours. As a result, whenever I looked in the mirror, I did not see my own reflection but rather the wicked, gloating eyes of its former owner, looking at me as though determined that I should be her next victim. I gave the mirror to Professor Ganesh Saili. He's immune to witches and spirits from the past.

I am a fearful, supernatural person, and I keep a horseshoe over my bed and a laughing Buddha on my desk. I love life, but I do not expect it to go on forever. Immortality is for the gods.

Judging from some of the movies I see on television, the Americans are obsessed with aliens, creatures from outer space who are immortal, indestructible. These are really projections of themselves, wishful thinking for they would love to be indestructible, forever young, perpetually in charge, running the show and turning us all into their own burger-eating images. Even now, there are scientists working on ways and means of extending human life indefinitely, even bringing the privileged few back from the dead. But nature has a few tricks of her own up her sleeve. Greater than human or alien is the underground force of nature that brings earthquake, tidal wave and typhoon to remind us that we are just puny mortals after all.

The pleasure, as well as the pathos of life, springs from the knowledge of its transitory nature. All our experiences are coloured by the thought that they may return no more. Those who have opted for perpetual life might find that the pleasure of loving has vanished along with the certainty of death. We are in no hurry to leave the world, but we like to know that there is an exit door.

It is rather like being a batsman at the wicket. He does not want to get out. When he has made his fifty, he strives to make his 100, and when he has made his 100, he is just as anxious to make 200. Who wouldn't want to be a Rahul Dravid or Tendulkar? But it is the knowledge that the innings will end, that every ball may be his last, that gives the game its zest. If you knew that you never could get out, that by some perversion of nature you were to be at the wicket for the rest of your life, you would turn round and knock the stumps down in desperation.

The other day, when I was having a coffee at a little open-air cafe on Rajpur Road, I noticed a heavily-built man, bald, limping slightly come in and sit down at an adjoining table.

There was something familiar about him, but it took me some time to place him. And then it was the way he raised his eyebrows and gestured with his hands that gave him away. It was an old schoolfellow, Nanda, who had been a star centre-forward in the school football team while I had been a goalkeeper. All of fifty years ago! The passing of time had left a criss-cross of rail and roadways across his cheeks and brows. I thought, 'How old he looks.' But refrained from saying so.

He looked up from his table, stared hard at me for a moment, recognized me, and exclaimed, 'Bond! After all these years... How nice to see you! But how old you look!'

It struck me then that the cartwheels of time had left their mark on me too.

'You look great!' I said with admirable restraint. 'But what happened to the knee?'

'All that tennis, years ago,' he explained. 'Made it to Wimbledon, if you remember.'

'Sure,' I said, although I'd forgotten. 'You athletic types usually give way at the knees.'

'You've got at least three chins now,' he commented, getting his own back.

'Bee stung me,' I said.

'Ha!'

After a further exchange of pleasantries and mutual insults, we parted, promising to meet again. But of course, we never did. Too many years had passed and we'd never really had much in common except football.

How does one keep the passing of time at bay? One can't, really. Ageing is a natural process. But some people age quicker than others. Heredity, lifestyle, one's mental outlook, all play a part. A merry heart makes for a cheerful countenance. That old chestnut still rings true.

And of course, it helps to stay active and to continue doing good work. An artist must not abandon his canvas, a writer his habit of writing, a singer his song...

About five years ago, there was a knock on my door, I opened it cautiously, hoping it wasn't another curious tourist, and in bounced a little man, looking rather like a hobbit, who clasped my hand, shook it vigorously and introduced himself as Mulk Raj Anand.

I was astounded. Here was one of the idols of my youth, a writer whose books I'd read while I was still at school. Alive and in the flesh!

I did not ask him his age. I knew he was ninety-five or

thereabouts. But of course, he was ageless. And brimming with ideas, curiosity, and joie-de-vivre. We talked for over an hour. When he left, he stuffed a note into Siddhartha's pocket. He was still writing, he told me, even if some of his work wasn't getting published.

This rather saddened me. Some of his finest novels (*The Big Heart*, *Seven Summer*, and others) were out of print, only *Untouchable* and *Coolie* were available. And this at a time when dozens of lesser talents were being published all over the place.

But that's the way of the world. You're up today and down tomorrow. Some of the finest writers of the last century —J.B. Priesdey, Compton Mackenzie, John Galsworthy, Sinclair Lewis—are neglected by today's publishers and literary pundits.

This is the day of the literary agent, and you don't get published abroad unless you are represented by one of these middlemen, who like to think they know what's good for the reading public. In India, we are fortunate to be without them. The relationship between publisher and author is still important. But Indian publishing is making great strides, and as authors start making more money, the agents will get into the act.

Where there's life there's hope (or is it the either way round?) and Mulk Raj Anand's confidence in the future and in his own skills give me hope. He has now touched his century, and although frail and in failing health, I am sure he reaches for his pen whenever the creative urge possesses him.

Creative people don't age. Their bodies may let them down from time to time, but as long as their brains are ticking, they are good for another poem or tale or song.

And what of happiness, that bird on the wing, that most elusive of human conditions?

It has nothing to do with youth or old age. Religion and philosophy provide little or no relief for a toothache, and we are all equally grumpy when it comes to moving about in a heat wave or getting out of bed on a freezingly cold morning. I am a happy and reasonably contented man when I am sitting in the sun after a good breakfast; but at 6.30 a.m. when I step onto the icy floor of the bathroom and turn on the tap to find the water in the pipe has frozen, I am not the cheerful person that people imagine me to be.

External conditions do play their part in individual happiness. But our essential happiness or unhappiness is really independent of these things. It is a matter of character, or nature, or even our biological make-up. There are prosperous, successful people, who are constantly depressed and miserable. And the less fortunate, those who must put up with discomfort, disability, and other disadvantages, who manage to be cheerful and good-natured in spite of everything. Some effort of course, is needed. To take life lightly and in good humour, is to get the most fun out of it. But a sense of humour is not something you can cultivate. Either you have it or you don't.

Mr Pickwick, with his innocent good nature, would be happy at any time or place or era. But the self-doubting, guilt-ridden Hamlet? Never.

If you have the ability, or rather the gift of being able to see beauty in small things, then old age should hold no terrors.

I do not have to climb a mountain peak in order to appreciate the grandeur of this earth. There are wild dandelions flowering on the patch of wasteland just outside my windows. A wild rose bush will come to life in the spring rain, and on summer nights the honeysuckle will send its fragrance through the open windows.

I do not have to climb the Eiffel Tower to see a city spread out before me. Every night I see the lights of the Doon twinkling in the valley below; each night is a festive occasion.

I do not have to travel to the coast to see the ocean. A little way down the Tehri road there is a tiny spring, just a freshet of cool, clear water. Further down the hill it joins a small stream, and this stream, gathering momentum joins forces with another stream, and together they plunge down the mountain and become a small river and this river becomes a bigger river, until, it joins the Ganga, and the Ganga, singing its own song, wanders about the plains of India, attracting other rivers to its bosom, until it finally enters the sea. So this is where the ocean, or part of it, began. At that little spring in the mountain.

I do not have to take passage to the moon to experience the moonlight. On full moon nights, the moon pours through my windows, throwing my books and papers and desk into relief, caressing me as I lie there, bathing in its glow. I do not have to search for the moon. The moon seeks me out.

There's a time to rove and a time to rest, and if you have learnt to live with nature's magic, you will not grow restless.

All this, and more is precious, and we do not wish to lose any of it. As long as our faculties are intact, we do not want to give up everything and everyone we love. The presentiment of death is what makes life so appealing; and I can only echo the sentiments of the poet Ralph Hodgson—

> Time, you old gypsy man,
> Will you not stay,
> Put up your caravan
> Just for one day?